Charles A. Briggs, Llewellyn J. Evans, Henry P. Smith

Inspiration and Inerrancy

Inaugural Address

Charles A. Briggs, Llewellyn J. Evans, Henry P. Smith

Inspiration and Inerrancy
Inaugural Address

ISBN/EAN: 9783337196288

Printed in Europe, USA, Canada, Australia, Japan

Cover: Foto ©Andreas Hilbeck / pixelio.de

More available books at **www.hansebooks.com**

INSPIRATION AND INERRANCY.

INAUGURAL ADDRESS BY

C. A. BRIGGS, D.D.,

Professor of Biblical Theology in Union Theological Seminary,
New York.

TOGETHER WITH PAPERS UPON BIBLICAL SCHOLARSHIP
AND INSPIRATION,

BY

LLEWELLYN J. EVANS, D.D.,

Professor of New Testament Exegesis in Lane Theological Seminary,
Cincinnati,

AND

HENRY PRESERVED SMITH, D.D.,

Professor of Hebrew in Lane Theological Seminary, Cincinnati,

AND AN INTRODUCTION BY

ALEXANDER BALMAIN BRUCE, D.D.,

Professor of Apologetics and New Testament Exegesis in the Free
Church College, Glasgow.

London:

JAMES CLARKE & CO., 13 & 14, FLEET STREET, E.C.

—

1891.

CONTENTS.

INTRODUCTION.

By A. B. BRUCE, D.D.,

Professor of New Testament Exegesis in the Free Church College, Glasgow.

INTRODUCTION.

THERE is no subject on which the religious public will at the present time more eagerly welcome a competent statement than, What to think about the Bible ? In all the churches it is a question, if not the question, of the hour. It is not a question merely, or even chiefly, as between believers and infidels, but among believers themselves; between men holding substantially the same creed regarding matters pertaining to religion; a question internal to faith, and dividing the household of faith. It is a question on which much discussion will be needed to bring about a good understanding between those who at present are divided in opinion and tempted to think evil of each other. And inasmuch as those who now stand opposed are really at one in their fundamental beliefs and aims, it is evidently very desirable that the debate should be carried on in a spirit of mutual respect and trust, and with the gravity and reverence that befit the theme.

One has only to pay a little attention to contemporary utterances of a representative character to be satisfied that discussion of the Bible question, as we may briefly call it, however undesirable in some respects, is unavoidable. In the late General Assembly of the Free Church of Scotland, one of the ablest, most scholarly, and most devout of the younger ministers of that church, in a debate on " Revision of the Confession of Faith," said : " The infallibility of the Scriptures is not a mere verbal inerrancy or historical accuracy, but an infallibility of power to save. The Word of God infallibly carries God's power to save men's souls. If a man submit his heart and mind to the Spirit of God speaking in it, he will infallibly become a new creature in Christ Jesus. That is the only kind of infallibility I believe in. For a mere verbal inerrancy I care not one straw. It is worth nothing to me ; it would be worth nothing if it were there, and it is not."

In the General Assembly of the Presbyterian Church of America, held about the same time, the report submitted on " Revision of the Confession," contained a proposal to add to the Confessional statement on the evidences that the Bible is the Word of God, a clause, including among these evidences " the truthfulness of the history and the faithful witness of prophecy and miracle." That is to say, the

American Committee of Revision appear to hold the historical accuracy—on which Mr. Denney, in the Free Church Assembly, set so little value—to be one of the marks of the Bible being a Divine Book, the absence of which would be fatal to its claims to be the Word of God. Here, surely, is a great cleavage in opinion—a chasm between two theological schools on a subject of vital importance which it were very desirable to have bridged over! It will serve no purpose to deny the cleavage, or to invent ambiguous formulæ to conceal it. The one thing needful is that each side in the controversy state its position as distinctly as possible, and do its very best to make good its case, and let the conscience of the Church, enlightened by discussion, decide on which side truth lies.

The two essays, by Professors Evans and Smith, of Lane Theological Seminary, now republished in England, are a valuable contribution to the literature of the controversy. They owed their origin to the "Briggs Case," of which we have already heard something, and shall ere long hear more. The American Presbyterian Church was set on fire, like the prairie, by the utterances of Professor Briggs, of Union Theological Seminary, New York, in his Inaugural Address, on the occasion of his transference to the new Chair of Biblical

Theology, founded by the munificence of the venerable Charles Butler, President of the Board of Directors connected with the Seminary. From one side of the continent to the other the Presbyteries were agitated by the question, Ought not the forthcoming Assembly to use its power of veto on the appointment of professors, and interdict the obnoxious professor from venting such opinions in the new Chair? The Presbytery of Cincinnati had to face the question like the rest, and Professors Evans and Smith were among the men of light and leading to whom the brethren looked for guidance in the crisis. The two papers now given to the British public were read before the Presbyterial Ministerial Association of Cincinnati, and thereafter published for general circulation. They have been received by American readers in many cases with cordial approval, and in all cases with respect, as statements emanating from men well entitled, both by their general standing and by their special studies, to address the public on the question at issue. It is believed that they will receive a not less cordial welcome on this side the Atlantic. Though they bear—in notes and in the form of expression—occasional marks of their origin, they are, in their main substance, of universal concern, and as well fitted to interest and instruct us here as the community for whose benefit they were primarily designed. The local element allowed to remain will rather add to, than detract from, the interest, as serving to give us some insight into the present phases of opinion in America on the subjects treated of.

Though the essays of the Lane professors may be regarded as independent contributions to current controversies concerning the Scriptures, they gain in importance when read in the light of the Inaugural Address of Professor Briggs, which was the innocent cause of all the turmoil that now disturbs the American Presbyterian Church. It has therefore been deemed advisable to include that Address in the present volume. The British public will, we are sure, be glad to have it in their power to make themselves acquainted with the utterances of a man who, formerly well and favourably known to theologians, has recently become famous as the object of ecclesiastical prosecution. The Address, which has for its formal theme *The Authority of Holy Scripture,* touches on several questions on which public opinion in America is very sensitive, such as the inerrancy of Scripture and the progressive sanctification of men after death. The larger portion of it, as was to be expected, is devoted to the important topic *The Theology of the Bible,* in connection with which the lecturer has much to say on the difference in spirit

between that theology and the theology of
dogmatic systems. Without going into detail,
it may be said that the tone of the discussion
is evangelic throughout, and that whatever of
a questionable character may be discovered in
the Professor's utterances, is really due to zeal
for the good cause of evangelic piety against
dogmatic legalism.

The two sides of the controversy are well
represented with Dr. Briggs, of Union Seminary, and Drs. Evans and Smith, of Lane,
as the advocates of modern views, and the
theologians of Princeton, with their well-known
conservative tendencies, acting as the accepted
and powerful champions of old orthodoxy.
The battle is indeed a very unequal one, so
far as numbers are concerned. The American
Presbyterian Church is still, as compared with
most of the British churches, in a state of
dogmatic slumber. The state of opinion there
to-day is something similar to that which prevailed here some thirty years ago. In the
Northern States theological conservatism is
in the ascendant, though not quite so strong
as the recent overwhelming vote against Dr.
Briggs might indicate; in the Southern States
it may be said to be in exclusive possession of
the field. The combatants on either side speak
and write with full knowledge of the situation.
On the one side there is the confidence inspired
by big battalions; on the other, the conscious-

ness that the advocate of new views takes his life in his hand. Happily, the sense of being in the minority does not seem to be very depressing in its effect on the American temperament. Our friends utter their thoughts with a due sense of responsibility, but without fear, and with the tone of men who have made up their minds for all possible consequences. The heroic temper of the War of Independence seems to be awaking, and we may expect to see some plucky fighting.

In the following pages frequent references occur to a joint article on Inspiration, by Professors A. H. Hodge and Warfield, which appeared in the pages of *The Presbyterian Review*, some ten years ago. It was a sort of manifesto of the Conservative Party, and it has the merit of bringing the question at stake to a definite point, and raising a clear issue. Specially noteworthy is the definition of Inspiration therein given. It is so important in its bearing on the controversy about the Bible that we deem it right here to quote the passage in which it occurs. It is as follows : "During the entire history of Christian theology the word ' Inspiration ' has been used to express either some or all of the activities of God co-operating with its human authors in the genesis of Holy Scripture. We prefer to use it in the single sense of God's continued work of superintendence, by which

—His providential, gracious, and supernatural contributions having been presupposed—He presided over the sacred writers in their entire work of writing, with the design and effect of rendering that writing an errorless record of the matters He designed them to communicate, and hence constituting the entire volume in all its parts the Word of God to us." Briefly, Inspiration is a contrivance for securing absolute inerrancy in the original autograph of Scripture. This is a fighting definition, and as such it will become more and more the idea of Inspiration prevalent in the Conservative camp. Whatever else Inspiration may be, or effect, the one thing certain and all-important, in the view of the advocates of unqualified inerrancy will be, that Inspiration insured that the Bible should possess that characteristic. What it is, in its own nature, how it operates on the human authors of the sacred books, they do not claim fully to know or feel bound to state; the one thing they profess to know about it is, that it has for its fruit an absolutely infallible book.

The definition is a very handy one for controversial purposes. It settles the question in dispute by begging it. The question is, Is absolute inerrancy a characteristic of the Scriptures, and those who maintain the affirmative start by defining Inspiration as a Divine superintendence which has for its

design and effect to secure an errorless record. By this definition those who maintain
the negative are put in the awkward position
of being obliged either to give up their con-
tention or to lie under the imputation of deny-
ing Inspiration. This method of settling a
controversy at a stroke by a definition is not
altogether new in the history of human
thought. It was the method by which Spinoza
established his system of Pantheism. The
whole superstructure of pantheistic thought
in the *Ethica ordine geometrico demonstrata*
rests on the definition of substance. "By
substance, I *understand*," says Spinoza, quietly,
"that which exists by itself, and is conceived
by itself." Of course, if this definition be
accepted, it follows that there is only one
substance—viz., God. In like manner the
authors of the tractate on Inspiration quietly
intimate that they "prefer" to use the term
Inspiration as denoting a superintendence
which insures an errorless record. If their
preference be allowed there is an end to the
question whether the record be errorless. The
method pursued in common by Spinoza and /
the Princeton theologians, for very opposite
purposes, reminds us of a subject given out by
the professor of mathematics in the University of Edinburgh to his class as a theme for
voluntary essays by the more adventurous
spirits. "Assume that the three angles of a

triangle are *not* equal to two right angles, and deduce the consequences." From the assumption certain members of the class, by irrefragable logic, deduced a considerable number of most preposterous propositions— a little system, in fact, of most absurd geo- metry. You can do anything in the way of reasoning, given the requisite assumptions and definitions.

An errorless Bible, " inspired " in the sense of being Divinely endowed with inerrancy, such is the watchword of one school; a Bible inspired in a much larger and more Divine sense than that of mere superintendence, but not necessarily inerrant, such is the position taken up by the rival school. It is a question of fact to be decided ultimately by an appeal to the Bible itself, and a careful inspection of all the relative phenomena. But it is not a mere question of fact for the advocates of inerrancy, but also of *faith;* for their position is that a single error, however minute, would ? be fatal to the claim of the Bible to be the Word of God. "A proved error," say Drs. Hodge and Warfield, " a proved error in Scrip- ture contradicts not only our doctrine, but the Scripture claims, and therefore its inspiration in making those claims. It is, therefore, of vital importance to ask, Can phenomena of error and untruth be pointed out?" Vital, indeed; and just because it is a matter of life

and death for them to make out that there
are no errors or mistakes in the Scriptures,
it becomes a matter of not less grave importance for their opponents to resist their con-
tention to the uttermost. It is the dogmatic
significance assigned to the presence or
absence of errors that makes the question at
issue one of the first order of importance.
In themselves the alleged errors in the Bible
may be very insignificant—mere spots on the
sun. But the smallest error in a date or a
number becomes a gigantic affair, if on it
depend the claim of the Bible to be the
Word of God, and its value as a guide in
faith and conduct. The solitary mistake then
becomes the symbol of a great principle, the
flag around which the army of the faithful
rally to fight to the death for the sacred Book
against its assailants, who would fain pass for
its devoted friends. For the real foes of the
Bible are those who stake everything on the
question of inerrancy. And its real friends are
those who strenuously assert that we are not
bound, under pain of losing our Bible, to hold
and prove against all comers that "all the
affirmations of Scripture of all kinds, whether
of spiritual doctrine or duty, or of physical
or historical fact, or of psychological or philosophical principle, are without any error when
the *ipsissima verba* of the original autographs
are ascertained and interpreted in their natural

and intended sense." And be it carefully noted, that it is only in refusing to come under such a tremendous obligation that the party represented by Professors Evans and Smith feel any zeal. They are nowise anxious to convict the Scriptures of errors—few or many, great or small. If all parties were willing to let inerrancy remain a mere question of fact, they would be glad to be relieved of the unwelcome task of discovering mistakes in the sacred page, and to devote themselves undistractedly to the more congenial occupation of searching into the treasures of spiritual wisdom hidden therein. Even the loudest assertion that there are no errors in the Bible would not provoke them to contradiction. They would be content that those who sincerely believe this should enjoy the comfort of their faith. But when believers in inerrancy, not content with enjoying their own faith, seek to impose it on others who cannot see with their eyes; when, besides maintaining that there are no errors in the Bible, they moreover maintain that there *cannot* be compatibly with its continuing to be the Word of God, and insist that this dogma shall be made a binding article of faith, and that the contrary opinion shall be treated as a heresy, then tame acquiescence is disloyalty to the cause, not only of Christian liberty, but of true reverence for the Bible.

In all controversies it is common for antagonists to try to show that the presumption is on their side, and that the *onus probandi* lies on their opponents. In this respect the advocates of inerrancy claim to have the advantage, alleging that the claims of Scripture itself, and the faith of the universal Church till recent times, and especially of those who have done most signal service to Christianity, are decidedly on their side. The question as to the *onus probandi* is seldom a vital one. The burden of proof always lies, or is righteously or unrighteously thrown, on those who are in the minority, or who represent new and unfamiliar opinions. It settles nothing as to the merits of the case. If those who refuse to swear by inerrancy are put upon their defence by an arrogant majority, confident of their orthodoxy, they need not break their hearts. As apologists, as bearers of that formidable burden, called *onus probandi*, they are in good company. Christ was put upon His defence by Pharisaism for the heinous crime of loving the sinful. Paul, as the Apostle of Gentile Christianity, and a Gospel of salvation on equal terms for all mankind, was put on his defence by Judaists, who insisted on the perpetual obligation of circumcision; and even by the eleven Apostles, who, though not Judaists, were far from sharing Paul's uncompromising zeal and generous enthusiasm for the liberties and privileges of Gentile believers. Both accepted their position with the meekness of wisdom, and offered apologies which made them, single-handed, stronger than a thousand supporters of use and wont, and converted views, which at first appeared heresies, into the universal creed of Christendom.

On a larger view of the situation, it is not so certain, as the advocates of inerrancy imagine, that the presumption is on their side. The analogy of God's ways in other departments of His providential action, suggests the intrinsic likelihood of His giving to men a religious guidance which, while amply sufficient, should not possess those ideal attributes which theorists might regard as indispensable. On this point Mr. Gladstone has written some wise words in his recently-published work on *The Impregnable Rock of Holy Scripture*—words all the more deserving of serious attention on the part of conservative theologians that in the main the writer is with them in his bias. "No doubt," he remarks, " there will be those who will resent any association between the idea of a Divine revelation and the possibility of even the smallest intrusion of error into its vehicle. This idea, however, is by no means altogether a novelty. It is manifestly included as a likelihood, if not a certainty, in the fact of continuous transmission by human means without continuous miracle to guarantee it. But, further, ought they not to bear in mind that we are bound by the rule of reason to look for the same method of procedure in this great matter of a written provision of Divine knowledge for our needs, as in the other parts of the manifold dispensation under which Providence has placed us? Now, that method or principle is one of sufficiency, not of perfection; of sufficiency for the attainment of practical ends, not of conformity to ideal standards; and the question what constitutes that sufficiency is a matter no more to be judged of by us, in relation to the Scriptures, than in relation to any other part of the Divine dispensations, on all of which the Almighty appears to have reserved His judgment to Himself." In taking up this wise ground Mr. Gladstone is confessedly the disciple of Bishop Butler. The lesson which the great author of *The Analogy* sought to teach — his contemporaries has not yet been fully mastered by religious people, especially in its bearing on the Scriptures. There is nothing to which devout minds are more prone than to taking charge of God's honour and reputation as an *Author*. Any Book having Him for its " Author " must, they think, possess all conceivable perfections—literary, moral, religious. Faults of any description in such a Book are not to be thought of—the mere imagination of

2

them were an impiety. If, in absence of any actual Bible, men were to set themselves to conceive what a Divine Book should be, taking for their guidance the principle of perfection in all possible respects, they would almost certainly form an idea very remote from the character of the Bible in actual existence. Professor Smith, in the beginning of his paper, illustrates what he calls "the natural theory concerning an inspired book" by the case of the Koran. The Mohammedans believe that the Koran was written in a perfect Arabic style, that every syllable is of directly Divine origin, that its text is incorruptible, and that it is the absolute authority, not only in religion and ethics, but also in law, science, and history. Having stated these and other facts relative to the Koran, Professor Smith goes on to remark: "The point I make is, This is the kind of Bible we should like to have God give us, and when we construct for ourselves a theory of revelation we do it along these lines." The value of his Essay largely lies in the illustrations it supplies from the history of theological opinion concerning the Old Testament, of the follies perpetrated by men who sought to settle on *à priori* principles, what a Bible should be. The story he tells about the vowel points of the Hebrew Bible is full of instruction and warning. Those who maintained that the vowel points of the Masoretic text belonged to the original autograph were acting in the same spirit as the men in our own day, who are the champions of Biblical inerrancy. They were acting as the self-elected guardians of God's reputation as an "Author." This habit of "patronising God" is a very inveterate one. It is as old as Job's friends, who constituted themselves the champions of Divine righteousness, and in their zeal maintained that no disaster ever overtook a really good man ; only to be called fools for their pains. When one thinks of those prosing friends of the afflicted saint he begins to see that the presumption probably lies in a different direction from what is commonly supposed. The likelihood is that the zealots for inerrancy are wrong. The self-elected champions of the Divine honour, the patronisers of God, have almost always been wrong. For, though men will persist in thinking the contrary, God's ways are not as our ways.

The case of the Hebrew vowels is, as is well known to Biblical scholars, not the only instance in which a misguided zeal for the honour of God, as an Author, has led theologians to take up untenable and demonstrably false positions. The controversy as to the characteristics of the Greek of the New Testament is another very instructive historical illustration of the folly of *à priori* reasonings in the interest of a foregone conclusion. The theorists said: The Greek of the New Testament must be pure, free of the vulgarisms of the spoken Greek of the time, and of Hebraisms in construction, otherwise God's credit as an Author would be compromised. The scholars, more concerned about facts than dogmatic theories, said, Both forms of corruption are traceable in the language of the Greek New Testament. There is no dispute about the matter now, and some, perhaps, would be glad to forget that there ever had been a dispute. But it is good to be reminded that there once was a time when it could not be said, as Drs. Hodge and Warfield say, with reference to their own time, that "no one claims that inspiration secured the use of good Greek in Attic severity of taste, free from the exaggeration and looseness of current speech, but only that it secured the accurate expression of truth, even (if you will) through the medium of the worst Greek a fisherman of Galilee could write, and the most startling figures of speech a peasant could invent." Every experience of this sort helps to strengthen the warning against *a-priorism*, and to suggest the thought that probably the dogma of inerrancy belongs to the same category of theological follies, as the dogmas of a vocalised Hebrew text, and a New Testament written in faultless Greek, and that it is simply the last enemy with which the spirit of inductive inquiry, *in re* the Bible, has to fight.

There does not appear to be any good reasons why this last enemy should not be combated with as little compunction as the other figments conjured up by the theological imagination. For one may well ask, *Cui bono,* the errorless original autograph, which no one has ever seen? This is a point which our readers will find very powerfully put by Professor Evans, in a passage too long to quote, but of which the opening sentences may here be given. "Everybody," he remarks, "will admit that in the process of transcription and transmission, at least, some error has crept into the book, some contradiction, some inaccuracy, which, as the matter stands, cannot be accepted as the exact statement of that particular matter. But is not that virtually to give up the whole position? What is Inspiration for? Surely to advantage the reader. But what is the value of an infallible editorship which does not secure a permanently infallible text?" These are questions, the force of which it is not easy to evade.

But the advocates of inerrancy may plead, If there was not once an errorless autograph then we have in the Scriptures no reliable guide, no infallible rule of faith and practice. Given an absolutely accurate autograph, no longer existing, indeed, but once existent, at least in successive parts of the sacred Book, then the problem is to work up to it, and get as near to it in our actual Bible as we can. We can, then, be sure that all in the actual Bible that cannot be suspected of having deviated from the autograph may be implicitly trusted as the very Word of God; and the residuum in which deviation has taken place— an insignificant portion of the whole, at the most—is always being reduced in amount by the labours of experts. But admit a single mistake, however minute, in the autograph, and uncertainty is introduced into the whole book. If, for example, the parts of Israel's history before, during, and after the sojourn in Egypt, were not correctly reported in the autograph copy of the Pentateuch, how can we be sure that the Prophets give us the true significance of that history, as the story of a people chosen by the God of the whole earth to give to the world the true religion? In short, the Bible cannot be trusted in anything unless it can be trusted in everything. It cannot be an infallible guide even in the most vital matters of religion, unless it be an infallible guide in matters of fact, date, or number.

It is difficult to conceive of reasoning like this proceeding from honest perplexity, and not from sheer wilfulness. The notion that the Bible can be no guide at all unless it be an absolutely infallible guide, is so entirely

contrary to our experience in other departments of human life. Can a father give no
useful guidance to a child, or a teacher to a
pupil, because he does not know everything,
and occasionally makes mistakes in his statements? Nay, is not the notion in question
contrary to experience, even within the sphere
of religion, and in connection with the use of
the Scripture as a guide? Is it not notorious
that men do get effective, practically infallible
guidance in faith and conduct from the Bible,
who do not conceive of it either in its actual
or in its ideal state as an infallible book?
Through use of the Scriptures many have
become men of God, thoroughly furnished for
all good work, for whom they have been
nothing more than a reliable source of information on the whole regarding the main
facts in the history of revelation, and a generally trustworthy guide in the interpretation
of the religious significance of the facts. Do
you with Thomas, wilfully say, Unless I put
my finger into the print of the nails I will
not believe; unless the original autograph was
absolutely free from error, I will have nothing
to do with the Bible? Because you have
seen, at least, with the eye of imagination,
the errorless autograph have you believed?
Blessed are they that have not seen and yet
have believed. Thank God the blessedness is
not rare. There are men who have believed

the Bible to be a Divine Book, and have got
from it all needful guidance, who have doubted
the canonicity of certain books, and so had
the use of only a mutilated Bible; who have
felt the full force of critical arguments against
the Mosaic origin of the Pentateuch, and the
exactitude of its historical narrations; who
have seen in the discrepancies between the
narratives in the books of Kings and Chronicles,
or in the Gospels, not mere difficulties taxing
the skill of the harmonist, but irreconcilable
contradictions; and who have found even in
the religious sentiments of the writers of the
Old Testament books, not a little with which
they were unable to sympathise—nay, from
which the perfect teaching of Christ seemed to
require them to dissent. And even of those
who now believe in an errorless autograph,
how many can honestly pretend that they
began to get good from the Bible only after
they had made up their minds as to its absolute infallibility, and had attained to intelligent and decided convictions on all questions
belonging to the departments of Biblical criticism and introduction? The errorless autograph was in most cases the end, not the
beginning, of their faith. Speaking generally,
the question of Inspiration, and all that it
involves, is a question *internal* to faith. Most
men are a good way on the road to heaven by
the grace of God, and the guidance of Jesus

Christ, who, more than even the Bible, is the true Leader of faithful souls, and Guide of those that travel to the skies, before they know well what to think on the thousand and one problems of Biblical science, or have any right to entertain a personal opinion on the subjects to which these relate. Perhaps they start on their heavenward journey with a provisional theory as to inerrancy; but it is not in consequence of holding that theory that they derive benefit from the sacred Book. It may be doubted, indeed, whether holding it does not do them quite as much harm as good, causing them to use the Bible mechanically as a blind guide of the blind, as if all parts of the volume were alike valuable, all statements alike words of God, and everything to be believed and done for which chapter and verse could be quoted.

The Bible is not such a mechanical rule of faith and practice as the devout, but ignorant, use just described, assumes. It is not a highway wherein wayfaring men, though fools, may walk and not err. Many wayfarers have erred grievously, not to say fatally. Think how the Rabbis and their disciples erred! They searched the Scriptures with commendable, almost pathetic, diligence, and they missed Christ. The Bible was an errorless Book for them as for many now. They, in fact, were the originators of the theory of inerrancy; yet it did not keep them from error—nay, as conceived and used by them, it was the very cause of their error. It was a blind guide to blind men, with the inevitable consequence. It is never anything else to those who are spiritually blind. To be a useful guide in religion, the Bible must be spiritually used by men whose eyes God hath opened. To be a guide to the full extent of possible usefulness, it must be used with great discrimination; for of all "rules" the Bible is the least mechanical, insomuch that it were better to discard the term altogether and adopt some more apt expression, seeing that it is so suggestive of the idea of mechanical use. The Bible, if a rule, is one of a very unusual sort. It is a rule that improves on itself, and advances from less to greater degrees of perfection. Revelation was progressive, and that implies much. It implies that in the earliest stages of revelation there were, not immoralities, indeed, but certainly crude moralities. The distinction just taken is important, and ought to be carefully made for the honour of Scripture and the guidance of its readers. Immorality is the breach of a recognised moral standard. Crude morality is conformity with a low moral standard. Of such crude morality there are numerous instances in the Old Testament, and no one can wisely or profitably use the Old Testament as a guide who does not understand this and constantly keep it in mind. The progressive character of revelation implies further that there are defective religious sentiments to be found in the utterances of Old Testament saints corresponding to the rudimentary stage of revelation under which they lived. Hence, for example, the Psalms cannot, without qualification, be regarded, as Drs. Hodge and Warfield would have us regard them, as "divinely-inspired records of religious experience authoritatively set forth as *typical and exemplary* for all men for ever." Even so orthodox a writer as Dr. Owen admitted that in respect of the vindictive element they are not exemplary for Christians, since "all our obedience, both in matter and manner, is to be suited to the discoveries and revelations of God to us." And if it be inquired what is to guide us in respect to what is typical and exemplary in Old Testament piety, and what not, the answer must be the teaching of Christ and His example as illustrative of that teaching, and the teaching of the Apostles as filled with Christ's Spirit. The New Testament must be our guide in a critical discriminating use of the Old. Christ and the New Testament have not done their work in us if they have not enabled us to read and use with due discrimination the utterances of Old Testament Psalmists and Prophets, so that we shall not take them as examples in their vindictiveness, their querulousness, their way of judging God's favour by outward events, and other defects incidental to the dispensation under which they lived.

The question, How to think of the Bible? now agitating the Churches, is not a mere question of the school. It has most important practical bearings on the interests of religion. This is a fact which it behoves both sides duly to lay to heart, and it may be admitted that the religious interest does not lie all on one side in this controversy. There are risks connected with the freer critical view of the Bible as well as with that to which it is opposed, the main risk being that in the prosecution of our studies of the Sacred Book, on modern methods, we may be tempted to forget that it is an exceptional book, not to be merged among the mass of sacred books, which have come down to us from ancient times. The best antidote to this evil is to make ourselves thoroughly acquainted with the religious books of other peoples; for the effect of a careful comparison is certainly to enhance our sense of the superlative, unique value of the Bible. But it belongs to the present connection of thought, and the aim we have in view in writing this introductory statement, that we should emphasize a truth less likely to receive credence—viz., that the strict traditional way of regarding the Bible has its own peculiar and serious dangers. Without attempting an exhaustive statement, we may specify two directions in which we are exposed to peril.

The anxious maintenance of the dogma of inerrancy tends to foster a legal attitude of mind in our whole way of thinking concerning God as the "Author" of the Bible, and concerning inspiration and the inspired writers, and the inspired products of their pens. We are apt to think of God as concerned for His dignity and reputation as an Author, of Inspiration as a matter of mere "supervision" with a view to secure minute accuracy, of the inspired writers as "scribes" rather than Prophets, and of the inspired writings as Rabbinical treatises rather than as the very antipodes of all that we are accustomed to associate with the name of Rabbinism. It surely does not need to be proved that all these conceptions are false and unwholesome! If any one needs to be taught the first principles concerning the oracles of God we refer him with confidence to Professor Evans, who, in his Essay, makes some admirable statements on the topics above mentioned. God, as the Author of Scripture, he represents not as a Being very much concerned about His dignity and reputation, but as revealing rather in the whole character of the Sacred Book His grace and condescension, coming so low down " that He is not ashamed to use bad grammar, is not afraid of a barbarism or a solecism, does not

shrink from an archaism or an anachronism."
With a just feeling that there is an officious
way of being jealous for God's honour which
really amounts to a profanation, he appeals to
his opponents not to "charge upon God the
priggish precision which makes as much of a
mole-hill as of a mountain," and assures them
that "God does not care to be honoured in
that way," and that He is not to be mistaken
for "an intolerant, if not intolerable, pedant
who insists on his p.'s and q.'s with no less
vigour and pertinacity than on His godlike
SHEMA, 'Hear, O Israel!' or on His everlasting AMEN, 'Verily, verily, I say unto you.'"
To certain ears this language may sound irreverent or almost blasphemous; but there is no
case in which use of strong language is better
justified than in exposing and denouncing
conventional, false, idolatrous reverences.

Nothing could be more fitted to mislead us
as to the nature of Inspiration than to lay the
emphasis on the supervision necessary to in-
sure perfect accuracy. To an unsophisticated
view this seems to be about the last thing
to be thought of in connection with that
mysterious subject. Whatever Inspiration is,
it is not, one would say, principally, if at all,
 a supernatural device for insuring accuracy.
Judging from analogous phenomena coming
within the range of observation, the inspired
condition would seem rather to be one which

produces a generous indifference to pedantic accuracy in matters of fact, and a supreme absorbing concern about the moral and religious significance of facts. The inspired man may be careful about his facts—it may ultimately turn out that the historical accuracy of Biblical statements is much greater than many critics at present are prepared to allow—but such exactitude is not the *raison d'être* of his inspiration. The inspired man is not a mere chronicler or historian, but one who, with true prophetic insight, can read the moral of history, and for that purpose a very moderate measure of historical accuracy will suffice. If the main outline of Israel's history be true, even though some of the details be legendary— the prophetic interpretation of it, as the story of an elect people, will stand.

The other evil springing out of the erection of the inerrancy dogma into an article of faith, is the baleful influence it exercises on the interpretation of Scripture. There are three types of interpretation, all alike bad, and to be shunned by all who value common sense and common candour. There is the allegorical interpretation of the Alexandrian Jews, which had for its aim to educe from the Hebrew Scriptures Greek Philosophy. There is the Rabbinical interpretation of the scribes which had for its aim to make out a connection between the oral and the written law, and attained its end by processes of reasoning, by means of which anything whatever could be shown to be taught in the Scriptures. Lastly, there is the interpretations of the *Harmonists,* which had for its aim to show that all passages of Scripture which seem to contradict each other are capable of reconciliation. The attempt to harmonise discrepant texts is in itself legitimate and useful, but to feel under an obligation in all cases to bring out harmony, and to make the reconciliation of discrepancies a canon of interpretation, is another matter. It means frequent jesuitry and occasional absurdity, in exegesis, and it diverts attention from the essential truth underlying discrepant narrations. As an instance of the grotesque absurdities into which a rigid harmonistic may lead, Professor Evans cites the case of Osiander finding it necessary to make Peter's wife's mother have fever, and be cured of it three times over. How much more satisfactory that she should be properly cured once for all!

The Gospels are the main theatre of harmonistic operations, and we cannot think without sadness of so much effort being wasted on the endeavour to bring the Evangelists into perfect accord in details, which might be more profitably expended in elucidating their grand common theme, the ministry of Love and the doctrine of the Kingdom. To the harmo-

nists busy at their petty task we are inclined
to say, Sirs, we would see Jesus. It may,
indeed, be thought that the minor work of
harmonising may be combined with the major
work of exhibiting the mind and spirit of
Christ. But it is not easy ; the moods that go
along with the two kinds of work are so
different. Theoretically, it may seem quite
practicable to combine scrupulous payment of
tithes, even on garden herbs, with due attention to the great matters of the law, justice,
mercy and faith. But a wide experience has
shown that zeal for minutiæ tends to undermine conscience, so that men who carefully
strain out gnats are too often equal to the feat
of swallowing camels. In like manner it may
be affirmed that it is not from the harmonists
that we have got, or are ever likely to get, good
" Lives of Jesus." To paint the image of the
Great Master successfully, one must be set free
from slavish solicitude about harmonistic problems, and feel at liberty to handle the materials
with a fearless breadth of treatment.

The Old Testament history also contains
phenomena of discrepancy which cannot be
profitably dealt with on harmonistic principles.
The question in reference to the Books of
Chronicles is not, How can their narratives be
reconciled with those of the Books of Kings ?
It is rather, What were the religious circumstances of the age in which the Chronicles

3

were written which account for these variations and help us to understand their moral lesson? This, however, cannot be gone into here, and it is the less needful to do so that the topic is handled by Professor Smith at considerable length and with sound judgment.

In conclusion, let us say that men create for themselves a great many difficulties in connection with Scripture by thinking of God too literally as an Author. Viewing the matter abstractly, it is difficult to understand how, if God be really the Author of the Bible in the same sense in which Milton was the author of *Paradise Lost,* He should not write in perfect style, and with perfect accuracy in all statements of fact, and in perfect accordance with the ideal standard in morals and religion. He is surely the most consummate Artist; He knows everything; He is absolutely holy. How can He possibly embody His thought in inferior Greek? How can He possibly make a mistake? How can He have anything to do with crude morality or a defective religious tone? To questions of this sort more might be added, such as that one asked by the free-thinker Reimarus, How could God, the Holy One, employ as His agents in revelation men with glaring moral infirmities? There are several ways of dealing with these questions. One is to deny the facts on which they are based: to allege boldly that the Greek is faultless ; that there are no mistakes in point of fact, no crude moralities, no religious shortcomings ; that all the men of revelation were faultless, saintly, perfectly exemplary persons. Another way is to admit the facts and draw from them the sweeping conclusion, There was no revelation, the Bible is in no sense an exceptional Book. The best way is to admit the facts and try to discover a way of reconciling them with the reality of revelation and inspiration. This can be done partly by conceiving of God's relation to the Bible as less immediate than was formerly supposed, and partly, and very specially, by giving large prominence to the gracious condescension of God in the whole matter of revelation. Think of God's authorship as spiritual, not literary; and remember that in giving to the world a Bible, through the agency of the best minds in Israel, He was greatly more concerned about showing His grace, than about keeping aloof from every form of human imperfection.

THE AUTHORITY OF HOLY SCRIPTURE.

By C. A. BRIGGS, D.D.,

Professor of Biblical Theology in Union Theological Seminary,
New York.

THE AUTHORITY OF HOLY SCRIPTURE.*

THE theme for my discourse to-night has sprung out of the necessities of the situation. It seems to be my duty to set forth my views fully and frankly with reference to those fundamental questions of our times that underlie the discipline of Biblical Theology. Accordingly, I have chosen that upon which everything depends—the Authority of Holy Scripture.

Human nature is so constituted that, when self-consciousness and reflection rise into activity, there is an irresistible impulse to seek authority for the relations in which we find ourselves, the knowledge that is taught us, and the conduct prescribed for us in life. We may be content as children with the authority of our parents, as young men and maidens with the authority of masters and teachers, but, sooner or later, the responsibility is thrown upon ourselves, and we alone must bear the strain of life, incur its

* Delivered as an Inaugural Address in Union Theological Seminary, New York, on the evening of Tuesday, the 20th January, 1891.

obligations, and earn its rewards and penalties for time and for eternity. What authority shall be our guide and comfort in life is a fundamental question for man at all times, but never has it been so urged upon our race as in the closing years of the nineteenth century.

If we undertake to search the forms of authority that exist about us, they all alike disclose themselves as human and imperfect, and we feel at times as if we were upon an unknown sea, with pilots and officers in whom we have no confidence. The earnest spirit presses back of all these human authorities in quest of an infallible guide and of an eternal and immutable certainty. Probability might be the guide of life in the superficial eighteenth century, and for those who have inherited its traditions, but the men of the present times are in quest of certainty. Divine authority is the only authority to which man can yield implicit obedience, on which he can rest in loving certainty and build with joyous confidence.

The progress of criticism in our day has so undermined and destroyed the pillars of authority upon which former generations were wont to rest, that agnosticism seems to many minds the inevitable result of scientific investigation. We cannot know God, we cannot be certain with regard to ultimate realities. Man cannot rise to the throne of the Deity. He cannot see the Invisible or know the transcendent. Unless God in some way enter within the region of human knowledge, we cannot know Him. But if God be God, if He be the Creator and Sovereign of the universe. if He has made it and governs it with a holy purpose, He may not only transcend universal nature by reigning over it, but He may enter into it, inhabit it, and pervade it with His immanence. He may disclose His presence in forms that men may be able to discern.

I.—THE SOURCES OF DIVINE AUTHORITY.

It is the testimony of human experience in all ages that God manifests Himself to men, and gives certainty of His presence and authority. There are historically three great fountains of Divine authority—the Bible, the Church, and the Reason.

(1.) *The Authority of the Church.* — The majority of Christians from the apostolic age have found God through the Church. Martyrs and saints, fathers and schoolmen, the profoundest intellects, the saintliest lives, have had this experience. Institutional Christianity has been to them the presence-chamber of God. They have therein and thereby entered into communion with all saints. It is difficult for many Protestants to regard this experience as any other than pious illusion and delusion.

But what shall we say of a modern like Newman who could not reach certainty, striving never so hard, through the Bible or the Reason, but who did find Divine authority in the institutions of the Church?* Shall we deny it because it may be beyond our experience? If we have not seen God in institutional Christianity, it is because the Church and its institutions have so enveloped themselves to us with human conceits and follies. Divine authority has been so encased in the authority of popes and councils, prelates and priests, ecclesiastics and theologians, that multitudes have been unable to discern it; and these mediators of redemption have so obtruded themselves in the way of devout seekers after God that they could not find God. Plain, common people have not been offended so

---

* " From the time that I became a Catholic, of course, I have no further history of my religious opinions to narrate. In saying this, I do not mean to say that my mind has been idle, or that I have given up thinking on theological subjects ; but that I have had no changes to record, and have had no anxiety of heart whatever. I have been in perfect peace and contentment. I never have had one doubt. I was not conscious to myself, on my conversion, of any difference of thought or of temper from what I had before. I was not conscious of firmer faith in the fundamental truths of revelation or of more self-command; I had not more fervour ; but it was like coming into port after a rough sea; and my happiness on that score remains to this day without interruption."—Newman's *Apologia Pro Vita Sua*, p. 264.

much by this state of things, because they are accustomed in all denominations to identify the authority of God with the authority of priest and pastor, as a child identifies the authority of the parent with the authority of God ; and men of deep spiritual insight may be able to force their way through these obstructions, and find God in spite of them. But to men of the temperament and environment of the average educated Protestant such an experience is difficult, if not impossible. Nevertheless, the Church is a seat of Divine authority, and the multitudes of pious souls in the present and the past have not been mistaken in their experience when they have found God in the Church.

(2.) *The Authority of the Reason.*—Another means used by God to make Himself known is the forms of the Reason, using Reason in a broad sense to embrace the metaphysical categories, the conscience and the religious feeling. Here, in the Holy of Holies of human nature, God presents Himself to those who seek Him. The vast multitude of men are guided by God through the forms of the Reason, without their having any consciousness of His presence or guidance. There are few who are able to rise by reflection into the higher consciousness of God. These few are of the mystic type of religion ; the men who have been the prophets of mankind, the

founders of religions, the leaders of Revivals
and Reformations, who, conscious of the
Divine Presence within them, and certain of
His guidance, lead on confidently in the
paths of Divine Providence. Such men have
appeared in all ages of the world. Some of
them have been the leaders of thought in
modern times in Great Britain, Germany, and
America. We ought not to be surprised that
they should depreciate the Bible and the
Church as merely external modes of finding
God, for even the prophets of the Bible attach
little importance to the institutions of Israel,
and seldom mention them, except to warn
against their misuse.*

It may be that these modern thinkers have
a Divine calling to withdraw men from mere
priestcraft, ceremonialism, dead orthodoxy and
ecclesiasticism, and concentrate their attention
on the essentials of the Christian religion.

Martineau could not find Divine authority in
the Church or the Bible, but he did find God
enthroned in his own soul.† There are those

---

* 1 Sam. xv. 22—23 ; Is. i. 10—17 ; Jer. vii. 22—26 ;
Mic. vi. 6—8.

† "Divine guidance has never and nowhere failed to
men; nor has it ever, in the most essential things, largely
differed amongst them; but it has not always been recognised as divine, much less as the living contact of
Spirit with spirit—the communion of affection between
God and man. While conscience remained an *impersonal*

who would refuse these Rationalists a place in the company of the faithful. But they forget that the essential thing is to find God and Divine certainty, and if these men have found God without the mediation of Church and Bible, Church and Bible are means and not ends; they are avenues to God, but are not God. We regret that these Rationalists depreciate the means of grace so essential to most of us, but we are warned lest we commit a similar error, and depreciate the Reason and the Christian consciousness.

(3.) *The Authority of Holy Scripture.*—We have examined the Church and the Reason as seats of Divine authority in an introduction to our theme, the *Authority of the Scriptures,* because they open our eyes to see mistakes

law, stern and silent, with only a jealous Nemesis behind, man had to stand up alone, and work out for himself his independent magnanimity; and he could only be the pagan hero. When conscience was found to be inseparably blended with the Holy Spirit, and to speak in tones immediately divine, it became the very shrine of worship—its strife, its repentance, its aspirations, passed into the incidents of a living drama, with its crises of alienation and reconcilement; and the cold obedience to a mysterious necessity was exchanged for the *allegiance of personal affection.* And this is the true emergence from the darkness of ethical law to the tender light of the life Divine. The veil falls from the shadowed face of moral authority, and the directing love of the all-holy God shines forth."—Martineau's *Seat of Authority in Religion,* p. 75.

that are common to the three departments. Protestant Christianity builds its faith and life on the Divine authority contained in the Scriptures, and too often depreciates the Church and the Reason. Spurgeon is an example of the average modern Evangelical, who holds the Protestant position, and assails the Church and Reason in the interest of the authority of Scripture. But the average opinion of the Christian world would not assign him a higher place in the Kingdom of God than Martineau or Newman. May we not conclude, on the whole, that these three representative Christians of our time, living in or near the world's metropolis, have, each in his way, found God and rested on Divine authority? May we not learn from them not to depreciate any of the means whereby God makes Himself known to men? Men are influenced by their temperaments and environments which of the three ways of access to God they may pursue. There are obstructions thrown up by the folly of men in each one of these avenues, and it is our duty as servants of the living God, to remove the stumbling-block out of the way of all earnest seekers after God, in the avenues most familiar to us.

No one of these ways has been so obstructed as the Holy Bible. The ancient Jews made a fence about the law, and enclosed it with circle upon circle of traditional interpretation, so that the law itself was hidden out of sight, the external circle of interpretation having taken its place, and the authority of God was obscured by the authority of man. The Christian Church pursued the same method, and concealed the Word of God behind the authority of popes and councils, fathers and schoolmen. The Reformers brought the Bible from its obscurity for a season, but their successors—the scholastics and ecclesiastics of Protestantism—pursued the old error and enveloped the Bible with creeds and ecclesiastical decisions, and dogmatic systems, and substituted for the authority of God the authority of a Protestant rule of faith. The Bible has been treated as if it were a baby, to be wrapped in swaddling-clothes, nursed, and carefully guarded, lest it should be injured by heretics and sceptics. It has been shut up in a fortress, and surrounded by breastworks and fortifications as extensive as those that envelop Cologne and Strasburg. No one can get at the Bible unless he force his way through these breastworks of traditional dogmatism, and storm the barriers of ecclesiasticism.

II.—THE BARRIERS OF DIVINE AUTHORITY IN HOLY SCRIPTURE.

The Bible is the book of God—the greatest treasure of the Church. Its ministry are messengers to preach the Word of God, and to invite men to His presence and government. It is pharisaic to obstruct their way by any fences or stumbling-blocks whatever. It is a sin against the Divine majesty to prop up Divine authority by human authority, however great or extensive. The sun is shining in noontide splendour. Lest men, by looking at it, should quench the light of the great luminary, let us build walls so high that they cannot see the sun, and let us guard its light by reflecting mirrors. The grace of God is the true elixir of life to all mankind. Lest indiscriminate use of it should vitiate its powers, let us dilute it in several degrees, so that it may not come to men directly, but only through a succession of safe hands. How absurd, you say. And yet this is the way men have been dealing with the Bible, shutting out the light of God, obstructing the life of God, and fencing in the authority of God.

(1.) *Superstition.* — The first barrier that obstructs the way to the Bible is *superstition*. We are accustomed to attach superstition to the Roman Catholic Mariolatry, Hagiolatry, and the use of images and pictures and other external things in worship. But superstition is no less superstition if it take the form of *Bibliolatry*. It may be all the worse if it concentrate itself on this one thing. But the

Bible has no magical virtue in it, and there is no halo enclosing it. It will not stop a bullet any better than a mass-book. It will not keep off evil spirits any better than a cross. It will not guard a home from fire half so well as holy water. If you desire to know when and how you should take a journey, you will find a safer guide in an almanac or a daily newspaper. The Bible is no better than hydromancy or witchcraft if we seek for Divine guidance by the chance opening of the Book.* The Bible, as a book, is paper, print, and binding—nothing more. It is entitled to reverent handling for the sake of its holy contents, because it contains the Divine word of

---

* I am far from any disposition to treat with disrespect the religious convictions of pious Roman Catholics or Protestants. Roman Catholic divines recognise that there are superstitious uses of the mass-book, the cross, and holy water, that are not justified by Roman Catholic doctrine and usage. My argument is against those Protestants who exhibit the same superstition toward the Bible as some Roman Catholics show in the ceremonies of their religion. Superstition is just as bad in the one as in the other. The only difference is in the forms of its manifestation. In my experience, those who make the loudest outcry against Roman Catholic superstition are the very ones who are most guilty of the superstition I am condemning in Protestantism. The criticisms that have been made upon this address, especially in religious journals noted for their hostility to Roman Catholicism, show that Bibliolatry is more prevalent in Protestantism than I had supposed.

redemption for man, and not for any other reason whatever.

(2.) *Verbal Inspiration.*—The second barrier, keeping men from the Bible, is the dogma of *verbal inspiration.* The Bible in use in our churches and homes is an English Bible. Upon the English Bible our religious life is founded. But the English Bible is a translation from Hebrew, Aramaic, and Greek originals. It is claimed for these originals by modern dogmaticians that they are verbally inspired. No such claim is found in the Bible itself, or in any of the creeds of Christendom. And yet it has been urged by the common opinion of modern evangelicalism that there can be no inspiration without *verbal inspiration.** But a study of the original languages of the Bible finds that they are languages admirably fitted by Divine Providence for their purpose,† but still, languages developing in the same way essentially as other human languages. The text of the Bible, in which these languages have been handed down, has shared the fortunes of other texts of other literature.

We find there are errors of transmission. There is nothing Divine in the text—in its letters, words, or clauses.‡   There are those

* Briggs, *Whither*, pp. 64 *seq.* Charles Scribner's Sons.
† Briggs, *Biblical Study*, pp. 42 *seq.* Charles Scribner's Sons.
‡ *Biblical Study*, pp. 156 *seq.*

who hold that thought and language are as inseparable as body and soul. But language is rather the dress of thought. A master of many languages readily clothes the same thought in half-a-dozen different languages. The same thought in the Bible itself is dressed in different literary styles, and the thought of the one is as authoritative as the other. The Divine authority is not in the style or in the words, but in the concept, and so the Divine power of the Bible may be transferred into any human language.* The Divine authority contained in the Scriptures speaks as powerfully in English as in Greek, in Choctaw as in Aramaic, in Chinese as in Hebrew. We force our way through the language and the letter, the grammar and the style, to the inner substance of the thought, for there, if at all, we shall find God.

(3.) *Authenticity.*—The third barrier is the *authenticity of the Scriptures.* The only authenticity we are concerned about in seeking for the Divine authority of the Scriptures is *Divine authenticity,*† and yet many theologians have insisted that we must prove that the Scriptures were written by or under the superintendence of prophets and apostles.‡ Refusing to build on the authority of the living

---

* *Whither,* p. 66. † *Biblical Study,* pp. 220 *seq.*
‡ *Whither,* pp 81 *seq.*

Church, they have sought an authority in the dead Church; abandoning the authority of institutional Christianity, they have sought a prop in floating traditions. These traditions assign authors to all the books of the Bible, and on the authority of these human authors, it is claimed that the Bible is Divine. These theologians seem altogether unconscious of the circle of reasoning they are making. They prove the authority of the Bible from the authority of its authors. But what do we know of the authors apart from the Bible itself? Apart from the sacred writings, Moses and David, Paul and Peter, would be no more to us than Confucius or Sakya Muni. They were leaders of men, but how do we know that they were called of God to speak Divine words to us? The only way in which we can prove their authority is from their writings, and yet we are asked to accept the authority of the writings on the authority of these authors. When such fallacies are thrust in the faces of men seeking Divine authority in the Bible, is it strange that so many turn away in disgust? It is just here that the Higher Criticism has proved such a terror in our times. Traditional-ists are crying out that it is destroying the Bible, because it is exposing their fallacies and follies. It may be regarded as the certain result of the science of the Higher Criticism that Moses did not write the Pentateuch or

Job ; Ezra did not write the Chronicles, Ezra, or Nehemiah ; Jeremiah did not write the Kings or Lamentations ; David did not write the Psalter, but only a few of the Psalms ; Solomon did not write the Song of Songs or Ecclesiastes, and only a portion of the Proverbs ; Isaiah did not write half of the book that bears his name. The great mass of the Old Testament was written by authors whose names or connection with their writings are lost in oblivion.* If this is destroying the Bible, the Bible is destroyed already. But who tells us that these traditional names were the authors of the Bible ? The Bible itself ? The creeds of the Church ? Any reliable historical testimony ? None of these ! Pure, conjectural tradition ! Nothing more ! We are not prepared to build our faith for time and eternity upon such uncertainties as these. We desire to know whether the Bible came from God, and it is not of any great importance that we should know the names of those worthies chosen by God to mediate His revelation. It is possible that there is a providential purpose in the withholding of these names, in order that men might have no excuse for building on human authority, and so should be forced to resort to Divine authority. It will ere long become clear to the Christian people that the

---

* *Biblical Study,* pp. 222 seq.

Higher Criticism has rendered an inestimable service to this generation and to the generations to come. What has been destroyed has been the fallacies and conceits of theologians; the obstructions that have barred the way of literary men from the Bible. Higher Criticism has forced its way into the Bible itself and brought us face to face with the holy contents, so that we may see and know whether they are Divine or not. Higher Criticism has not contravened any decision of any Christian council, or any creed of any Church, or any statement of Scripture itself. It has rather brought the long-neglected statement of the Westminster Confession into prominence:

"The authority of the Holy Scripture, for which it ought to be believed and obeyed, dependeth not upon the testimony of any man or church, but wholly upon God (who is truth itself), the author thereof; and therefore it is to be received, because it is the Word of God."*

Luther, with keen spiritual insight, once said:

"What does not teach Christ, that is not apostolic, even if St. Peter or St. Paul taught it: again, what preaches Christ, that would be apostolic, even if Judas, Annas, Pilate, and Herod did it."†

* Confess. of Faith, I. 4.
† Köstlin, *Luther's Theologie*, II. 256; Walch. xiv., p. 149.

It used to be the fashion to apologise for this word of Luther; but here, as elsewhere, Luther was truer to the Gospel than modern theologians.

(4.) *Inerrancy.*—The fourth barrier set up by theologians to keep men away from the Bible is the dogma of the inerrancy of Scripture. This barrier confronts Historical Criticism. It is not a pleasant task to point out errors in the sacred Scriptures. Nevertheless, Historical Criticism finds them, and we must meet the issue whether they destroy the authority of the Bible or not. It has been taught in recent years, and is still taught by some theologians, that one proved error destroys the authority of Scripture.[*] I shall venture to affirm that, so far as I can see, there are errors in the Scriptures that no one has been able to explain away; and the theory that they were not in the original text is sheer assumption, upon which no mind can rest with certainty.[†] If such errors destroy the authority of the Bible, it is already destroyed for historians. Men cannot shut their eyes to truth and fact. But on what authority do these theologians drive men from the Bible by this theory of inerrancy ? The Bible itself nowhere makes this claim. The creeds of the Church nowhere

---

[*] *Biblical Study*, pp. 240 *seq.*; *Whither*, pp. 68 *seq.*
[†] *Whither*, p. 72.

sanction it. It is a ghost of modern evangelicalism to frighten children. The Bible has maintained its authority with the best scholars of our time, who with open minds have been willing to recognize any error that might be pointed out by Historical Criticism;* for these errors are all in the circumstantials and not in the essentials ; they are in the human setting, not in the precious jewel itself ; they are found in that section of the Bible that theologians commonly account for from the providential superintendence of the mind of the author, as distinguished from divine revelation itself. It may be that this providential superintendence gives infallible guidance in every particular ; and it may be that it differs but little, if at all, from the providential superintendence of the fathers and schoolmen and theologians of the Christian Church. It is not important for our purpose that we should decide this question. If we should abandon the whole field of providential superintendence so far as inspiration and divine authority are concerned and limit divine inspiration and authority to the essential contents of the Bible, to its religion, faith, and morals, we would still have ample room to seek divine authority where alone it is essential, or even

* G. P. Fisher, *Nature and Method of Revelation*, p. 206 *seq.* ; Charles Gore, in *Lux Mundi*, pp. 354 *seq.* ; W. Sanday, *Oracles of God*, pp. 15 *seq.*

important, in the teaching that guides our devotions, our thinking, and our conduct. Whether divine authority extends to the circumstantials of this divine teaching or not, it is unwise and it is unchristian to force men to accept the divine authority of the Bible or reject it, on the question of its inerrancy in the circumstantials and the details of every passage.*

(5) *Violation of the Laws of Nature.*—The fifth obstruction to the Bible has been thrown up in front of modern science. It is the claim that the *miracles* disturb, or violate, the laws of nature and the harmony of the universe; and so the miracles of the Bible have become to men of science sufficient evidence that the Bible is no more than other sacred books of other religions.† But the theories of miracles that have been taught in the Christian Church are human inventions for which the Scriptures and the Church have no responsibility whatever.

The miracles of the Bible are confined to the life of Christ and His apostles and to the ministry of Moses, Elijah, and Elisha, with very few exceptions. The Biblical writers do not lay so much stress upon them as modern apologists. Moses and Jesus both warn their disciples against miracles that would

---

* *Whither,* p. 73.   † *Whither,* pp. 279 seq.

be wrought in the interest of false prophets and false messiahs.* The tests that they gave to discriminate the true from the false were not their marvellous character, their violation of the laws of nature, their suspension of the uniformity of law or the comprehension of extraordinary laws with ordinary laws in higher laws—nothing of the kind; but the simple test whether they set forth the holy character and the gracious teaching of God and His Messiah. The miracles of the Bible are miracles of redemption. They exhibit the love of God and the compassion of the Messiah for the needy, the suffering, and the lost. † These divine features of Biblical miracles have been obscured by the apologists, who have unduly emphasized their material forms. The miracles of the Bible were the work of God either by direct divine energy, or mediately through holy men, energized to perform them; but there is no reason why we should claim that they in any way violate the laws of nature or disturb its harmonies. We ought not to be disturbed by the efforts of scholars to explain them under the forms of divine law, in accordance with the order of nature. If it were possible to resolve all the

* Deut. xiii. 1-5; Matth. xxiv. 24-28 ; 2 Thess. ii. 8-12.

† A. B. Bruce, *The Miraculous Element in the Gospels*, pp. 258 *seq.*

miracles of the Old Testament into extra-ordinary acts of Divine Providence, using the forces and forms of nature in accordance with the laws of nature; and if we could explain all the miracles of Jesus, His unique authority over man and over nature, from His use of mind cure, or hypnotism, or any other occult power,—still I claim that nothing essential would be lost from the miracles of the Bible; they would still remain the most wonderful exhibition of loving purpose and redemptive acts of God and of the tenderness and grace of the Messiah's heart. Christian men may construct their theories about the miracles of the Bible with entire freedom so long as they do not deny the reality of the events themselves as recorded in Holy Scripture. The study of the miracles of the Bible has convinced me that they may be explained from the presence of God in Nature, in various forms of Theophany and Christophany, for where God is present we may expect manifestations of divine authority and power. As my friend, Dr. Bruce, recently said:

" Miracles are not the effects of partially or wholly unknown physical causes; they are produced by immediate divine causality. But they are not on that account lawless or unnatural. They are wrought for a worthy end, and in accordance with a wise plan. They are natural in the sense that they are congruous to the nature of God, falling within the compass of

His power and subject to the direction of His wise,
holy, loving will. They are natural further, I may add,
in the sense that they do not wantonly interrupt or
upset the order of nature, but rather put it to higher
uses, which from the first it has been fitted and
destined to subserve."—Bruce's *The Miraculous Element in the Gospels*, p. 66.

(6) *Minute Prediction.*—Another barrier to
the Bible has been the interpretation put upon
Predictive Prophecy, making it a sort of history
before the time, and looking anxiously for the
fulfilment of the details of Biblical prediction.
Kuenen has shown that if we insist upon
the fulfilment of the details of the predictive
prophecy of the Old Testament, many of these
predictions have been reversed by history;
and the great body of the Messianic prediction
has not only never been fulfilled, but cannot
now be fulfilled, for the reason that its own
time has passed for ever.*

The Book of Jonah gives valuable suggestion here. See Jonah going to Nineveh with
a prediction that in forty days Nineveh will
be destroyed, and then going to a safe place
outside the city, waiting with impatience for
the grand sight, the destruction of the metropolis of the world. But Nineveh repents, and
God recalls His decree, and the city is spared.
The prophet is so distressed and humiliated at

* Briggs, *Messianic Prophecy*, pp. 43 *seq.* Charles Scribner's Sons.

the failure of his prediction that he longs for death.* Doubtless, God has not fulfilled His prediction. He has recalled it. The messenger has been discredited as a predictor, but he has been accredited as the channel of the redemption from God. It may be that Nineveh will presume upon the weakness of God, His fickleness and changeableness. But at all events, God Himself takes the risk. This is not the only unfulfilled prediction in the Old Testament. God has recalled more than one of His messages of woe.† He postpones the *dies iræ* until men count Him slack in the fulfilment of His promises, and mock and jeer at His justice.‡

They know not that their salvation is involved in these recalls and postponement. God is not willing that any should perish. He rules over the world to redeem as many as possible. This makes it difficult for a hard and fast system of dogma. It troubles the apologist and disarranges his lines of defence, but it presents God Himself as the God of man, the very God that humanity craves. Jonah represents only too well the general attitude of Jew and Christian alike to the heathen world. Embedded in Jonah, un-.noticed save by Zwingli and a few Anabaptists

* Jonah iii., iv.

† Is. xxxviii.; Briggs, *Messianic Prophecy*, pp. 58 *seq.*

‡ 2 Peter iii. 3--9.

and heretics, is the gospel of infant salvation
and of heathen salvation.

"Should not I have pity on Nineveh, that
great city, wherein are more than six-score
thousand persons that cannot discern between
their right hand and their left hand, and also
much cattle?"*

We need no evidence that this is a Divine

---

* Jonah iv. 11. I recently came upon a passage in one
of the early Baptists, using this verse of Jonah in a way
that was unknown to orthodox circles:

"And our Saviour Christ Luke XVIII: 16. in commenda-
tion of the condition and qualitie of Babes, saith, *Suffer
the Babes to come unto Me: for of such is the kingdome of
Heaven.* And Matth. XVIII: 3. *Except ye be converted and
become as little children ye shal not enter into the kingdome of
heaven. & Ver. 4 whosoever therefore shal humble himself as
this little child, the same is the greatest in the Kingdome of
heaven.* In all this shewing, that the children of Christ's
Kingdome must be off such humble qualities and conditions
as infants, & I hope none will deny, but al infants are off
one quality & condition, even the infants of the Turks, our
Saviour speakes off al infants generally: & evil men yet
judge some infants condemned.

"And of such infants the Lord sheweth his great com-
pasion, when he saith to the Prophet Jonah—Jonah IV. 11
. . . . whereby the Lord sheweth that they had not
sinned, neither were giltie off their Fathers sinnes. And
wil you yet charge the Lord to condemne so manie infants
and al for Adams sinne? are not your waies unequall thus
to say and teach me to hold & think off God?"—Tho.
Helwys. *A Short and Plaine Proof by the Word, and workes
off God that Gods decree is not the cause of anne Mans sinne or
condemnation. And that all men are redeemed by Christ. As
also that no Infants are condemned.* 1611, sine loco.

utterance; it speaks for itself. It is clearer than a thousand detailed predictions and their fulfilment.

We have passed through these barriers that men have thrown up in front of the Word of God, the breastworks against Philosophy, History, and Science. It is not surprising that multitudes of the best men of our age have rejected a Bible thus guarded and defended, as if it could not sustain the light of day. Doubtless there are many who are thinking that the critics are destroying the Bible. They have so identified these outworks with the Bible itself that *their* Bible vanishes with these barriers. I feel deeply for them. But we have a right to assume that if these apologists are within the camp of God, they ought to have such confidence in Divine authority that nothing from without could shake them.' If they have been relying on the defences and too little upon the Bible itself, it is high time that they were forced back to the Bible. But I feel more deeply for those many men, honest and true, whom they have been keeping away from the Bible.* I would say to all such: We

---

* Dr. A. B. Bruce, one of the keenest observers of the religious life of our times, says: "I certainly believe that there are many more unpolished diamonds hidden in the churchless mass of humanity than the respectable church-going part of the community has any idea of. I am even disposed to think that a great and steadily-increasing por-

have undermined the breastworks of traditionalism; let us blow them to atoms. We have
forced our way through the obstructions; let
us remove them from the face of the earth,
that no man hereafter may be kept from the
Bible, but that all may freely enter in, search
it through and through, and find God enthroned in its very centre.

Here in the citadel of the Bible two hosts
confront the most sacred things of our religion
—the one the defenders of traditionalism,
trembling for the ark of God; the other the
critics, a victorious army, determined to capture
all its sacred treasures and to enjoy all its
heavenly glories.

The self-constituted defenders can no longer
retain a monopoly of the Word of God and
exact conditions of all who would use it. It
has already been taken from them by Biblical
criticism, and it is open to all mankind, without conditions. Is it not their heritage? Did
not Jesus and His apostles offer it to them as
glad tidings of redemption to the world? Are
there not treasures of grace in Holy Scripture
amply sufficient for all mankind? It is the
teaching of God that men are anxious to know;
the theology of the Bible itself is what they

tion of the moral worth of society lies outside the Church,
separated from it not by godlessness, but rather by excep-
tionally moral earnestness. Many, in fact, have left the
Church in order to be Christians."—*Kingdom of God*, p. 144.

are craving. The teaching of men and the theology of creeds and theologians no longer content them. These all have their place and importance, but they cannot take the place of the theology of the Bible and the authority of God.

III.—THE THEOLOGY OF THE BIBLE.

We are now face to face with *Biblical Theology.* Here, if anywhere, the Divine authority will be found. It is my habit to divide Biblical Theology into three sections— Religion, Doctrines of Faith, and Morals. Let us look at the God of the Bible as He discloses Himself in some of these forms.

A.—*The Religion of the Bible.*

(1.) *Theophanies.*—The most prominent feature of the religion of the Bible is Theophany. Theophanies are the bases of every advance, the fountain of prophecy, the source of miracle. They guide the heroic leaders and reformers of the Old Testament religion. A permanent Theophany guides Israel from Egypt to the Holy Land, and takes possession of the Holy Tabernacle and Temple as its permanent abode.*

* Briggs, *Biblical History,* pp. 16 *seq.* Charles Scribner's Sons.

Theophanies cluster about the Messiah at His advent, until these give place to the Christophanies, which are the great feature of the New Testament religion.

It is conceded that these Theophanies have features in common with the mythological conceptions of the ancient religions of the world, which have been rejected as mythical by historical criticism. But so soon as we compare the Theophanies of the Bible with heathen mythology, we observe striking differences.

(*a*) There is nothing of a polytheistic character about the Theophanies of the Bible. The one God manifests Himself to chosen men and a chosen people.

(*b*) The Theophanies of the Bible are not confined to ancient times, the legendary basis of the history; they pervade and control the entire history of the Bible.

(*c*) The mythological conceptions of the Divine presence are connected with gross conceptions, in which the gods are of like passion with ourselves; but the Theophanies of the Bible are pure and holy, and ever have in view the redemption of men. God assumes the forms of light or fire, or of angel or man, in order that He may be manifest to the human senses, and assure mankind of His presence and favour.[*]

[*] Briggs, *Biblical History*. p. 21.

(*d*) When the doctrine of the Divine trans-
cendence was unduly emphasized, the Theophanies remained in obscurity behind the
miracle and the prediction which might be
wrought by the power of God from a distance,
outside His universe. But now that the Immanence of God is rising into prominence,
the Theophany casts the miracle and the prediction into its shadow. We now know that
God is not only over all, but through all and
in all. He is not far from any one of us. If
we feel after Him we may find Him. We
cannot escape from His presence. If God
is really present in the world, pervading it,
inhabiting it, was it not a part of the Divine
instruction that men should be taught by
visible signs to see it and know it? When
He appeared to the ancients in human form
they were assured by their senses of His
ability to be with them in every hour of
need, and they were prepared for the conception of the great prophet of the exile: "I
dwell in the high and holy place, with him
also that is of a contrite and humble spirit."*
When God guided Israel by a pillar of cloud
and fire, He taught them in sensible signs the
sublime truth of His governance of mankind.
When He took up His abode in the Temple,
He was training them for the conception of the

* Is. lvii. 6.

universal religion, that He inhabits the whole earth. If God is really present in His world, and has an interest in the bearers of redemption to a chosen people, the kingdom of priests for mankind, is it not reasonable that He should show His form in the midst of the elements of nature, and ·His countenance in the faces of intelligent beings?

The Theophanies of the Old Testament lead on to the Christophanies of the New Testament—the incarnation, ascension, and advent in glory, whereby the Messiah taught mankind the great lessons of redemption. And the Theophany of the Divine Spirit at Pentecost was a visible and audible pledge of His permanent residence in the Church during the era of grace. If mankind needed additional theophanies, doubtless they would be given by the God of all grace; but those recorded in the Bible, from Genesis to the Apocalypse, make a royal highway of light and glory throughout Biblical history, and give sufficient assurance of the presence of the Triune God with the people of God until the end of the age, and the accomplishment of the destinies of the world and man.

(2.) *The Institutions of the Old Testament.*—
The institutions of the Old Testament religion are of a most elaborate character. Whatever theory we may hold as to their origin and development, whether given by Moses at the

basis of the history, or from a long series of prophets and priests during the history, they present a majestic system. About the throne-room of God, where the theophanic presence dwelt, were gathered sacred places, sacred furniture, sacred times, sacred orders of priest-hoods, rites of sacrifice and purification, and holy rules for life and conduct. These doubt-less belong to the region of external religion, and to a lower stage in the religious training of man. The Old Testament prophets knew as well as we that they were mere forms, invalid without holy contents of grace, that God dwells not in temples made by hands, the heavens cannot contain Him in all their wondrous heights and breadths; * obedience was ever more sacred than sacrifice,† and all the beasts of the forests were God's; the cattle gathered in thousands upon the hills, how could men satisfy Him with one of the flock or herd?‡ Pure hearts were vastly more important than clean hands.§ The universal priesthood of Israel‖ was older and more important than the Levitical and Aaronic orders.

This magnificent religious system is pure and holy throughout. A holy God can be

---

* 1 Kings viii. 27. † 1 Sam. xv. 22, 23.
‡ Ps. l. 8—14.
§ Is. i. 10—17; Ps. xxvi. 6. ‖ Ex. xix. 5—6.

worshipped only by a holy people, and in ceremonies of holiness. Hence, there was not, and could not be, any of the cruelty, licentiousness, intemperance, and manifold vices that were inseparably entwined in the institutions of the other great religions of the world. Divine institutions are forms of grace, dignity, and beauty, to set forth the wonders of redemption. They point forward, as by myriad flames of light, to the Messiah, who absorbs them in the sunshine of His presence. They then pass away as the shades of the night, when first they see the eyelids of the dawn.* They become, for all ages and all men, the appropriate symbols of the universal religion. They evince by their history and their realisation that God had for a season clothed Himself with these forms and ceremonies for the enlightenment and guidance of mankind.

B.—*The Faith of the Bible.*

The Faith of the Bible embraces the three topics : God, Man, and Redemption.

(1.) *The Doctrine of God.*—The God of the Bible is *one* God, not merely the God of a family, a tribe, a land, a nation, but the God of all the earth. It is true, Israel learned this only by degrees—but nowhere in the Bible do

---

* Col. ii. 17.

we find any recognition of other gods as having a place in a pantheon. God is sovereign of angels, seraphim and cherubim, of the hosts of heaven, as well as of Israel and mankind. The God of the Bible is *spirit*—He transcends the universe that He created, governs and directs it to its appointed end, but He is immanent in His universe, inhabiting it and by His energy shaping all its forces. The God of the Bible is a *person*, bearing proper names, the most significant of which, Jahveh, indicates his personal interest in, and guidance of, His people, a person who may be approached in prayer and praise, and who recognises His worshippers, bestowing upon them blessings of every kind. The God of the Bible is a *living* God, the fountain of every life and activity, living in all life, moving in all motion.

The Being of God in the Bible is still high above the best attainments of philosophical theism, and the most skilful constructions of the systematic theologian. When we turn from the best of them to the God of the Bible, it is like rising from earth to heaven. A new doctrine of God is one of the greatest needs of our time.* The Bible gives it to us if we will only look at it and embrace it.

How was it possible for any ancient writer to have conceived or imagined such a God,

* Briggs, *Whither*, pp. 93, *seq.*

unless God had presented Himself to him in the forms of the Reason, and he had seen and known Him as the only living and true God?

The attributes of God as set forth in the evolutions of Biblical Theology have none of those faults that appear more or less in ¦the best system of Theology.* That God is just, righteous, a God of equity and judgment, is as clear as the day. The great sovereign of the earth must do justice; we need no Bible to tell us that. But the favourite attribute of the Old Testament and the New is the attribute of mercy, because this attribute man needs most to know, and it is not so evident in the light of nature. The mercy of God is the theme upon which the histories and the prophets, the singers and the sages alike delight to dwell. The greatest of the theophanies granted to Moses was in order to reveal God as the gracious, compassionate, the long-suffering, abounding in mercy and faithfulness.† The love of God rises to its heights in the fatherly love of Deuteronomy,‡ and the earlier Isaiah § and Jeremiah; ‖ in the marital love of Hosea,¶ Zephaniah, and the second Isaiah **—a love to an unfaithful

* Briggs, *Whither*, pp. 95 *seq.*   † Ex. xxxiv. 6-7.
‡ Deut. iv. 37; vii. 13; x. 15; xxxii. 6 *seq.*
§ Is. i. 2. *seq.*   ‖ Chap. xxx.-xxxi.
¶ Chap. i.-iii.   ** Is. liv. 1-17 lxii.

wife, who has disgraced her husband and herself by many adulteries; * and a child who rewards the faithful father with such persistent disobedience, that he must be beaten to death and raised from the dead in order to be saved.†
The love of God as taught in the Old Testament is hard for the Jew or the Christian to understand. It transcends human experience. It seems so impossible even for God, that men must be explaining it away. These wonderful chapters of the Old Testament are neglected in all of our creeds and systems of divinity—because these all exaggerate the Divine justice and veracity, and fear lest God should be too merciful. Like Jonah, they have not been able to conceive how it is possible for God to redeem the great cities of heathendom. They have not seen that He could have any compassion on the Samaritans and the Moabites, who do not belong to the Israel of God, but are the enemies of the historic faith.‡ They have seen the throne of God and its pillars of righteousness and justice, and have supposed that sovereignty was enthroned there. They have not seen the *love* that was seated on the throne, and its messengers of mercy and

---

* Hos. i.-ii.

† Jer. xxxi. 18-20; Hos. xi. 8, 9; xiii. 14.

‡ *How shall we revise the Westminster Confession of Faith?* pp. 98 *seq.* Charles Scribner's Sons.

faithfulness going forth with salvation to the children of men.*

The love of God as taught in the Old Testament transcends human powers of conception. None could have taught such love who had not seen the loving countenance of God, and experienced the pulsation of that love in their own hearts. The love of God in the Bible is an invincible, a triumphant authority that invokes the loving obedience of men.

It is not necessary to depreciate the love of God in the Old Testament in order to exalt the love of the Messiah. The love of God in the Old Testament is the preparation to understand the love of God in the New Testament, who so *loved the world*, as to give His only begotten Son for its salvation.† O, when will men learn that the Bible means exactly what it says! It may destroy *our* logic and *our* syllogism, *our* systems and *our* methods. These we have too long regarded as authorities. Logic and syllogism, system and method, need constant criticism, verification and revision ; for too often they omit the essential thing. Their inductions are too narrow, their comprehension is too limited ; they beg their premises and jump to their conclusions. The love of God to the world is more important than all the systems devised by men. It will

---

* Ps. lxxxix. 14.   † John iii. 16.

shine for ever as the central sun of the universe, when all the creeds and theologies have been buried in the oblivion of the eternities. It will go on through the centuries of the world, darting its rays of heavenly light, its beams of Divine fire, and its regenerating and transforming movements, until the world knows that God loves the world, and the world adores Him with loving worship.

(2) *Doctrine of Man.*—The doctrine of Man in the Bible is Divine doctrine. A twin mirror shows man what he is in sin and misery, and what he is to be in holiness and happiness.

The Word of God is a revelation of the sin of man. Sin is exposed in the interests of redemption, that it may be brought to the consciousness of every reader of the Bible. The conscience approves the voice of the Spirit saying, " Thou art the man,"* when our sins disclose themselves in the picture gallery of the Bible, and we are convicted before the internal tribunal by a Divine voice speaking with an authority that cannot be questioned, bringing us to temporal judgment, that we may escape the ultimate doom.

The Bible presents sinful man in the midst of an original innocency and an ultimate perfection. Sin is only a temporary condition. Jew and Christian alike exaggerate the original

* 2 Sam. xii. 7.

innocency and depreciate the ultimate perfection.* The exaggeration of the original innocency is in the interest of an original righteousness, which, like a dress, might be removed as a punishment of sin and then put on again by grace.

Protestant theologians have exaggerated the original righteousness in order to magnify the guilt of our first parents. They thus come in conflict with ethical and religious philosophy. The Bible is not responsible for these exaggerations. The original man was innocent and sinless, but not possessed of that righteous and moral excellence that comes only by discipline and heavenly training. The temptation was a necessary means of grace. Man did not make his religious progress in the straight line of faith and obedience, but in the curved line of sin and redemption.

But the most important thing in Biblical Anthropology is the ideal of mankind. Man was created to be the lord of nature, the culmination of its evolutions. Man was made to be God-like ; and though he sought it in the paths of disobedience, he is sure to gain it on the highway of redemption. Man was *one* in origin, and cannot be any other than *one* in the plan of God.† The processes of re-

* Briggs, *Whither*, pp. 107 *seq.*
† Briggs, *Messianic Prophecy*, pp. 69 *seq.*, 476 *seq.*

demption ever keep the *race* in mind. The
Bible tells us of a race origin, a race sin, a race
ideal, a race redeemer, and a race redemption.*

These ideals of the Bible are high above
reality. They are so grand and glorious that
they have been persistently misunderstood and
perverted by men. None of us rise to their
transcendent glories.

God holds these twin mirrors before us to
drive us from sin and to compel us to holiness.
Divine authority in the Bible calls to every one
of us: Forsake sin and live a perfect life ; come
unto Me and be My son, My holy one, the
child of My good pleasure.

---

* No one can understand the doctrine of the Incarnation
who does not conceive of a relation of the Messiah to the
race. My revered teacher, Henry B. Smith, says: " The
destiny of man in Christ is to come to the measure of the
stature of his fulness. Christ is the very ideal of humanity
realized. Even in a human point of view, He is the
consummate flower of the human race, a character unique
in wisdom, love, and holiness. Not only in the individual
life and individual perfection does the relation subsist
between man and Christ, but it also holds of man as a
whole, of the collective race, of man in history. We are *all*
to come into the unity of the faith and knowledge of the
Son of God . . . . He who gives the law to history is
the law-giver of the race. In Him, and in Him alone, the
secrets of humanity are hid, its enigmas resolved, its sal-
·vation insured. He who redeems the race must be the
Head and Lord of the race. The whole human family finds
its centre, its crown, its peace, in Him."—*System of Christian Theology,* pp. 383-4.

(3.) *Redemption*.—Redemption is born of the love of God ; it aims at the transformation of the sinful and suffering race of man into the image of God. It comprehends the whole nature of man, his whole life, and the entire race. The history of the world is the Divine discipline of mankind.

(*a*) The Old Testament doctrine of Redemption is chiefly concerned in the material interests of man. In the vast majority of cases it has to do with salvation from enemies, from afflictions and sorrows, from poverty and from death. Our Saviour's ministry was chiefly to the poor and the outcasts in Israel, the publicans and the harlots ; and the redemption that He gave them was not merely the forgiveness of sins, but redemption from physical sufferings. The Christianity of Christ is to heal the sick, to feed the hungry, to give drink to the thirsty, to comfort all that mourn. Such are the tests that the Messiah applies in His royal judgment, whether His servants have followed His example in doing just these things in their ministry.*

The Redemption taught in the Bible aims to remove all the ills that flesh is heir to. There can ·be no Darkest Africa or Darkest London which the light of Redemption may not illuminate with heavenly influences. Poverty,

* Matt. xxv. 31-46.

vice and crime are inconsistent with Christianity. Christianity has undertaken to remove them from the world. The Bible gives us the principles, the examples, and the Divine authority for their extirpation. Christianity is inconsistent with the present social condition of New York, and the other great cities of the world. We have no right to the name of Christians; we bring reproach on the name of Jesus Christ; we dishonour the God of the Bible, and are stumbling-blocks in the way of the suffering multitudes, obstructing their way to God, and their entrance into the kingdom of heaven, if we do not, with all our souls, strive to relieve their misery and want. The Bible, through and through, insists upon the redemption of the bodies of men, as well as their souls, and of the whole framework of human society. This heavenly teaching is so against the prejudices and the attainments of mankind that it is an unmistakeable evidence of the Divine authority of the Scriptures that so strongly urge it upon us.

(*b*) The Redemption of the Bible comprehends the whole process of grace. Modern Protestants have unduly emphasized the beginning of redemption, justification by faith alone.* The slight put upon Christian love prevented many a devout soul, like Staupitz, from joining

* Briggs, *Whither*, pp. 142 *seq.*

in the Reformation. One of the disciples of Luther taught that good works were hurtful to salvation; and a practical, if not a theoretical, Antinomianism has too often been one of the Adam's apples of Protestantism.

James has a word for the men of this generation—Faith without works is dead.* A justification that does not lead on to sanctification gives no credentials of genuineness. A faith that does not result in a life of repentance discredits itself.

The movement called Methodism laid too much stress upon the experience of regeneration at the beginning of the Christian life.† But a regeneration that does not exhibit a real, earnest Christian life, fruitful in good works, is not a regeneration into the kingdom of God, whatever else it may be.

The Bible rises high above the faults of modern theology, and comprehends in its redemption of man his justification, sanctification, and glorification; his regeneration, his renovation, and his transformation; his faith, his repentance, and his holy love. No one who is not entirely saved can sustain the judgment of the day of doom.‡ If this Biblical doctrine could be impressed upon the men of our day,

---

* James ii. 26.   † Briggs, *Whither*, pp. 118 *seq.*

‡ 1 Thess. iii. 13; 1 Cor. i. 8; Rom. viii 29, 30; Eph. iv. 13-26.

the *authority* of God would disclose itself in a transformation of the world, and the introduction of an era in which holiness would be the aim of mankind.

(*c*) Another fault of Protestant theology is in its limitation of the process of redemption to this world,* and its neglect of those vast periods of time which have elapsed for most men in the Middle State between death and the resurrection. The Roman Catholic Church is firmer here, though it smears the Biblical doctrine with not a few hurtful errors. The reaction against this limitation, as seen in the theory of second probation, is not surprising. I do not find this doctrine in the Bible,† but I do find in the Bible the doctrine of a Middle State of conscious higher life in the communion with Christ and the multitude of the departed of all ages ; ‡ and of the necessity of entire sanctification, in order that the work of redemption may be completed.§ There is no authority in the Scriptures, or in the creeds of Christendom, for the doctrine of immediate sanctification at death. The only sanctification known to experience, to Christian orthodoxy, and to the

---

* Briggs, article *Redemption after Death*, in *Mag. of Christian Literature*, Dec., 1889. See also *Whither*, pp. 206 *seq.*

† *Whither*, pp. 217 *seq.*

‡ 2 Cor. v. 1-9; Heb. xii. 22-24, &c.

§ Matt. v. 48; John xvii. 17; Rom. viii. 29, 30; 1 John iii. 2.

Bible, is progressive sanctification.* Progressive sanctification after death is the doctrine of the Bible and the Church; and it is of vast importance in our times that we should understand it, and live in accordance with it. The bugbear of a judgment immediately after death and the illusion of a magical transformation in the dying hour† should be banished from the world. They are conceits derived from the Ethnic religions, and without basis in the Bible or Christian experience as expressed in the symbols of the Church. The former makes death a terror to the best of men, the latter makes human life and experience of no effect; and both cut the nerves of Christian activity and striving after sanctification. Renouncing them as hurtful, unchristian errors, we look with hope and joy for the continuation of the processes of grace and the wonders of redemption in the company of the blessed, to which the faithful are all hastening; and through these blessed hopes we enter into the communion of all saints, and have a happy consciousness of the one holy Catholic Church, whose centre and majestic frame are chiefly in the skies, the one body of the one Christ.

(*d*) The Biblical redemption is a redemption of our race and of universal nature. The Bible

---

* *West. Confession*, chap. xiii.   † *Whither*, p. 195.

teaches that the material universe shares in the destiny of man, and is in throes of birth for this blessed hope.* As the ancient Jews limited redemption to Israel and overlooked the nations, so the Church limited redemption to those who were baptized, and excluded the heathen and the unbaptized; and Presby-terians have too often limited redemption by their doctrine of Election. The Bible knows no such limitations. The Bible teaches election, but an election of love.† Loving only the elect is earthly, human teaching. Electing men to salvation by the touch of Divine love—that is heavenly doctrine. The one drives men away in despair, the other unites men with joy to the love of God.‡ The Bible does not teach universal salvation, but it does teach the salvation of the world, of the race of man, and that cannot be accomplished by the selection of a limited number of individuals from the mass. The holy arm that worketh salvation does not contract its hand in grasping only a few; it stretches its loving fingers so as to comprehend as many as possible—a definite number,

---

* Rom. viii. 18—25.   † *Whither*, pp. 95 *seq.*

‡ "Election is the expression of God's infinite love towards the human race, redeeming man from sin through Christ, and by the Holy Spirit bringing him into this state of redemption, so far as it is consistent with the interest of God's great and final kingdom."—H. B. Smith, *System of Christian Theology*, p. 505.

but multitudes that no one can number. The
salvation of the world can only mean the
world as a whole, compared with which the
unredeemed will be so few and insignificant,
and evidently beyond the reach of redemption
by their own act of rejecting it and hardening
themselves against it, and by descending into
such depths of demoniacal depravity in the
Middle State, that they will vanish from the
sight of the redeemed as altogether and irre-
deemably evil, and never more disturb the
harmonies of the saints.

C.—*Biblical Ethics.*

We are now prepared for the *Ethics of the
Bible*, the fruitage of Theology, the test of
all the rest.   Biblical Ethics present us an
advancing system of morals—God showing
His holy face and character and the sublime
precepts of morality as men were able to bear
them.

In the field of Biblical Ethics there is considerable criticism at the present time. Biblical
Ethics have not been so carefully studied as
Biblical Religion and Biblical Faith; therefore the principles that determine their development are not so clearly understood.   There
is ample room for criticism in the ethical
precepts and in the conduct of the holy men
of the Bible.

The ancient worthies, Noah and Abraham, Jacob and Judah, David and Solomon, were in a low stage of moral advancement. Doubtless it is true, that we would not receive such men into our families, if they lived among us and did such things now as they did then. We might be obliged to send them to prison, lest they should defile the community with their example. But they do not live now; they lived in an early age of the world, when the Divine exposition of sin was not so searching, and the Divine law of righteousness was not so evident. They were not great sinners to their age; they were the saints of God.

Abraham was the father of the faithful,* the great hero of faith for all time, and it is an honour for a Christian to count him as father. When he went into the abode of the dead, he held his pre-eminence among the departed. He made up for his defects in this life by advancing in the school of sanctification there open to him. Let us not suppose that we have passed beyond him in sinlessness or ethical elevation. Our blessed Lord sees the poor Lazarus in Abraham's bosom, the synonym of Paradise itself.†

Jacob was crafty and treacherous, but he was a pilgrim to the Holy Land, one whose whole ambition was set upon the holy places,

---

* Rom. iv. 16—17.　　　† Luke xvi. 23.

one who is the father of all pilgrims, one who, therefore, gave his name to the Holy Land and to the entire Israel of God.

We should look more at their saintly characters that have given them their place among the heroes of the faithful. Thus we would trace the moral development of Israel, and see it advancing through the centuries until it reaches its height in the holy Messiah.

It has been too much the custom to use the ancient heroes of the faith as examples to rebuke modern sinners. They ought to be held up as examples to make modern heroes. And so it has been thought that Israel was a nation chiefly remarkable for its stiff neck and stubborn heart, for its unfaithfulness and its apostasy. Not so do we read in the Old Testament. Israel was the people of God, dearly beloved, and faithful in the main, ever advancing, never attaining the ideal. I fear that the Christian Church does not present so good a history as the people of Israel in the olden time. If Israel did not live up to the ethical principles of Moses and the Prophets, have we lived up to the ethics of Jesus and His Apostles? It is just this feature of Biblical Ethics that assures us that Divine authority is in it. It presents an ideal ever far above historical reality.

The Ten Words rise before us in majesty

as the guide of morality for the Christian Church, and are as authoritative as when first uttered by a Divine voice from Sinai.

. Most of the ethical provisions of the Pentateuchal codes were local and temporal validity, but there are many principles in them that are invaluable hints for the solution of the social problems of our day. There are ethical precepts in the Psalter and the Prophets, and, above all, in the Wisdom Literature of the Old Testament, that we need to study and to know. It is a very significant fact that this Wisdom Literature of the Old Testament which is essentially ethical, has been so neglected by theologians. The Book of Proverbs, the Book of Job, the Song of Songs, and Ecclesiastes are the masterpieces of Old Testament ethics. No portion of the Old Testament is likely to prove more useful in the ethical age upon which we are now entering. The holy God calls holy men into His service :

Who of us can abide with devouring fire?
Who of us can abide with everlasting burnings?
One walking in perfect righteousness, and speaking
    uprightly,
Refusing the spoil of oppression,
Shaking his palms from holding a bribe,
Shutting his ears from hearing of bloodshed,
And closing his eyes from seeing evil.*

If the ethical parts of the Old Testament

* Is. xxxiii. 15 *seq.*

have been neglected, this is still more the case with the ethical parts of the New Testament. It has been said that Calvinists come to a halt in a certain chapter of the Epistle to the Romans, but it may also be said that the Arminians come to a halt but a short distance further on.   Neither Calvinist nor Arminian has risen to the ethical heights of the closing chapters of the epistles to the Romans and the Ephesians.   The Epistle of James is ethical throughout ; it has not been a favourite epistle for Protestants.   The Epistles of John have been too high in their mystic elevation for the modern world.

But the greatest sin against the Bible has been the neglect of the ethics of Jesus.   If one studies the theology of Jesus he is impressed by the fact that it is profoundly ethical, not only in the Sermon on the Mount, but also throughout His discourses.   The holy man, living such a holy life, how could it be otherwise than that holy words were ever on His lips ?   Those who question the historicity of the life of Jesus, and regard many of His teachings as misunderstood by the Evangelists who report them, stand in awe and bow in adoration when they consider His ethical precepts and recognize their divinity.

Tolstoi says Christians think that Jesus did not mean what He said.   Tolstoi's criticism is severe, but is it not just ?   If we really believed that Jesus meant what He said, how could we live such selfish lives? The words of Jesus are so high above us that it seems impossible to realize them in actual life, and so we strive to get a meaning out of them that will be useful to us, and we bury the sublime ideal in a fictitious and temporary explanation.* It is my opinion that if the grace of God should so impel a man that he could be transformed into the image of the holy Jesus, and, like Jesus, rebuke sin in high places and trouble the people with his unapproachable holiness, he would earn the reward of Jesus even in this generation—at the hands of Chris-

---

* "The ecclesiastical Christ is to a large extent not the Christ of the Gospels, but a creation of scholastic theology. Notwithstanding all our preaching, Jesus Christ is not well known. That He is not well known is partly the fault of our preaching. Men are not permitted to see Jesus with open face, but only through the thick veil of a dogmatic system. The religious spirit of Jesus, His attitude towards the religion in vogue in Judæa in His time, and its grounds, His humane sympathies, His thoughts of God, His ethical ideal, have been allowed to fall into the background. Hence types of piety have sprung up within the Church, which, whatever virtues they may possess, are not characteristically Christian. It has become possible to be very religious and yet be very unchristian, not only largely ignorant of Christ, but antagonistic to Him in spirit; to be, in short, a modern reproduction of the Pharisee, imagining one's self to be one of the most faithful friends of Jesus, while hostile to all the true Christian interests of the time."— A. B. Bruce, *Kingdom of God*, p. 348. 4th Ed.

tian theologians and ecclesiastics. The cry would resound through the streets of New York, " Crucify him ! crucify him ! "

The words of Jesus, like the life of Jesus, are the ideals of perfection, that men thus far have been unable to understand and realize ; but they will be realized when the world has been so trained and disciplined in the progress of sanctification that it shall become like Him.

D.—*The Messiah.*

Thus far we have spoken of the Messiah only indirectly ; but every line of religion, doctrine, and morals has brought us unto Him. The Messiah is the culmination of the Old Testament. He is the pivot of History. All through these nineteen centuries Christians have been learning from their Lord, and yet how little do we know of Him. Each period in the history of the Church has been so deeply impressed with some small portion of what the Scriptures have revealed about Him, that it has devoted itself exclusively to that, has exaggerated that, and left other equally important phases of the doctrine unexplored.

Sometimes the deity of Christ has been so exalted that men have forgotten His humanity. Then others have been so absorbed in the wonders of His humanity that they have not seen His divinity. Then the complex nature, the union of the human and divine in the Theanthropos,—the profoundest minds of the Christian centuries have thought upon it and unfolded some of its glories, but it is still like the very heavens for heights of mystery and glory. The Messiah's state of humiliation has so absorbed men that they have neglected His state of exaltation and glory. In His state of humiliation modern Protestants have absorbed themselves in the crucifixion and death, and the doctrine of the Atonement involved therein. The wondrous doctrine of the Incarnation has been neglected until recent times.* It was the merit of my beloved teacher, Henry B. Smith, that he made *Incarnation in order to Redemption* † the structural principle of his theology. The holy life of Jesus, long neglected, has in recent years been studied as never before. But the Messiah's descent into the abode of the dead—a doctrine of great importance to the ancient Church ‡—His resurrection—His enthronement—His reign of grace—His second advent—O, how these have been neglected !

The Messianic idea of the Old Testament and the Christology of the New Testament are vastly fuller and richer, and grander than any

---

* *Whither*, pp. 112 *seq.*
† Henry B. Smith, *System of Christian Theology.*
‡ See *Redemption after Death. Mag. Christ. Lit.*, Dec. 1889.

one has imagined. The Christ of the Bible will exert a much greater power upon the coming generations when they grasp the full Biblical doctrine and cease expending their strength and exhausting their energies in the speculative elaboration of some few of its phases.*

In all departments of Biblical Theology there are new life and new doctrine and new morals for the Church of God. More light is about to break forth from the Holy Scriptures upon the Christian world,—light for all the churches, for all men, for all nations. The old methods of building on selected texts and isolated passages, which you will find in all the creeds and in all the dogmatic systems,† is about to pass away. The inductive study of the Bible forces us to study every word, sentence, and clause, and rise in the inductive process, until the whole organism of the Bible is presented to us. Such study of the Bible, so far as I have been able to pursue it, has made it to me the freshest, the newest, the most wonderful of Books; has brought about in my mind a different conception in every department of Theology. And many of those things that once seemed to be probabilities on the basis of speculative theology and confessional theology

* *How shall we Revise?* pp. 20 *seq.*
† *How shall we Revise?* pp. 137 *seq.*

have, in the light of God's Word and in the conviction of Divine authority, come to be certainties—the verities of God.

I have not departed in any respect from the orthodox teaching of the Christian Church, as set forth in its official creeds. I have had the inestimable privilege of learning, as a student and a friend, from two of the greatest Systematic Theologians of our century—Henry B. Smith and Isaac A. Dorner. These built upon the Bible and the Creeds, the History of Doctrine and the highest attainments of the Human Reason. Such Systematic Theologians the Church greatly needs at the present time, and no one can value them and their work more than I do. These never set up their systems as tests of orthodoxy. They renounce scholasticism and dogmatism. For the dogmatism of mere traditional opinion and of the dogmaticians, I have no respect. Their speculations are worthy of no more consideration than the speculation of other scholars. But for the Creeds of Christ's Church I have the greatest respect, for I am one of those who believes that God inhabits His Church and guides it in its official decisions, not inerrantly in every utterance, but in the essential doctrines in which the universal Church is in concord. But the theology of the Creeds marks only the consensus of attainment of the Church in the several stages of advance in the History of

Doctrine. They are far below the Biblical ideal, and, therefore, the best of them seems to give us such a small theology when set in the length and breadth, the heights and depths of the theology of the Bible.

As I have recently said, "Christian churches should go right on in the lines drawn by their own history and their own symbols; this will in the end lead to greater heights, in which there will be concord. Imperfect statements will be corrected by progress. All forms of error will disappear before the breath of truth. We are not to tear down what has cost our fathers so much. We are rather to strengthen the foundations and buttresses of the buildings as we build higher. Let the light shine higher and higher, the clear, bright light of day. Truth fears no light. Light chases error away. True orthodoxy seeks the full blaze of the noontide sun. In the light of such a day the unity of Christendom will be gained."*

IV.—THE HARMONY OF THE SOURCES OF DIVINE AUTHORITY.

I have endeavoured to lead you through the obstructions that confront the student of the Bible into the Holy Word itself, that you might recognise the authority of God in the Religion,

* *Whither*, pp. 297-8.

Faith, and Morals of the Bible. I must now ask you to go back with me, and use the advantages we have gained for a brief review of those other seats of Divine authority—the Church and the Reason.

If God really speaks to men in these three centres, there ought to be no contradiction between them. They ought to be complementary, and they should combine in a higher unity for the guidance and the comfort of men. It is my profound conviction that we are on the threshold of just such a happy reconciliation. The discrepancies that men have found have not been in the authority of God Himself, or in the essential principles that have enveloped it, but in those formal and circumstantial things upon which human nature in its weakness and its depravity ever lays so much stress. Removing these human conceits and follies and these obstructions erected by well-meaning but misguided men from the Bible, the Church, and the Reason, it will be manifest that they *are*, they *always have been*, and they always *will be* harmonious.

It is human folly to set the Bible against the Church, or either or both of them against the Reason. Whenever this is done, the opposition is only in the human forms and settings. It is clear to me that the Bible needs the Church and the Reason ere it can exert its full power upon the life of men.

Institutional Christianity was established by
Christ and His Apostles, and no one can safely
ignore it. It is the need of our time in that
advance toward Church Unity that we are
about to make, and to make with so much
energy and decision. It is necessary that we
should know what Institutional Christianity
really is, that we should be members *of the
visible Church* and share in the sacrifices and
triumphs of the Kingdom of God. The Bible,
from the very nature of the case, leads us
through its forms into the presence-chamber
of God, but our minds are filled at the same time
with the historic forms of the ancient world.
It is the office of the Church, in the use of its
institutions, to bring us into communion with
the Triune God in the forms of the modern
world, and give us the assurance of His presence with the Church through its history, and
with us in the hour and moment of our use of
its institutions. The Church unites with the
Bible in giving us the assurance of God's
presence and authority throughout History,
Christian as well as Hebrew, and of His
gracious help in the present. It gives us the
blessed experience of the communion of saints.
It opens the eyes to see that we are in the
outer ranks of innumerable lines of the host of
the living God, ever on the march through the
life in this world into the gates of Paradise and
onward on the highway of holiness to the

throne of God and the Lamb which ever bounds the horizon of the beatific vision. The neglect of the Church as a means of grace retards the use of the Bible itself as a means of grace and dulls our sensitiveness to the presence of God.

The Reason also has its rights, its place and importance in the economy of Redemption. I rejoice at the age of Rationalism, with all its wonderful achievements in philosophy. I look upon it as preparing men to use their reasons in the last great age of the world. Criticism will go on with its destruction of errors and its verification of truth and fact. The human mind will learn to know its powers and to use them. The forms of the reason, the conscience, the religious feeling, the æsthetic taste—all the highest energies of our nature, will exert themselves as never before. God will appear in these forms, and give an inward assurance and certainty greater than that given in former ages. These increased powers of the human soul will enable men to search those higher mysteries of Biblical Theology that no theologian has yet mastered, and those mysteries that are wrapped up in the institutions of the Church, to all who really know them. It is impossible that the Bible and the Church should ever exert their full power until the human Reason, trained and strained to the uttermost, rise to the heights of its energies, and

7

reach forth after God and His Christ with absolute devotion and self-renouncing love. Then we may expect on the heights of theological speculation, and from the peaks of Christian experience, that those profound doctrines that now divide Christendom by their antinomies will appear as the two sides of the same law, or the foci of a Divine ellipse, which is itself but one of the curves in that conic section of God's dominion, in which, in loving wisdom, He has appointed the lines of our destiny.

Go out into the country in the late winter or early spring, and you will see, everywhere, great activity. The farmers are at work with axe, and saw, and knives, the instruments of destruction, cutting off the limbs of trees, and pruning vines and bushes, and rooting out weeds; fires are running over the fields and meadows, the air is filled with smoke, and it seems as if everything were going to destruction. But they are destroying the dead wood, dry and brittle stubble, and noxious weeds. They are removing them out of the way of the life that is beating beneath the surface of the ground and throbbing in tree and bush. In a few days the fields will be mantled in living green, the trees and bushes will wave their leaves joyously, and deck themselves with blossoms of every variety of beauteous form and colour, and the world will rejoice in a new springtime. Thus is it at the present time in the higher world of religion and morals. Criticism is at work with knife and fire. Let us cut down everything that is dead and harmful, every kind of dead orthodoxy, every species of effete ecclesiasticism, all merely formal morality, all those dry and brittle fences that constitute denominationalism, and are the barriers of Church Unity. Let us burn up every form of false doctrine, false religion, and false practice. Let us remove every incumbrance out of the way for a new life; the life of God is moving throughout Christendom, and the springtime of a new age is about to come upon us :—

Let the wilderness and the solitary places be glad,
And let the desert rejoice, and let it blossom as the
    rose;
Let it blossom abundantly, and let it rejoice,
Even with joy and singing;
The glory of Lebanon has been given unto it,
The excellency of Carmel and Sharon;
They see the glory of Jahveh,
The excellency of our God.
Strengthen ye the weak hands,
And confirm the feeble knees.
Say to the fearful of heart, Be strong,
Fear not : behold your God,
He cometh with vengeance, with a Divine recompense
He cometh to save you.—(Isai. xxxv. 1-4.)

BIBLICAL SCHOLARSHIP AND INSPIRATION.

I.

By LLEWELLYN J. EVANS, D.D.,

Professor of New Testament Exegesis in Lane Theological Seminary Cincinnati.

BIBLICAL SCHOLARSHIP AND INSPIRATION.

IT is the purpose of this discussion to present
some of the accepted conclusions of the best
Christian scholarship of the day respecting
certain features of our sacred Scriptures, as
these conclusions bear on the question of the
inspiration, infallibility, and authority of these
Scriptures, and on the rights and obligations
of those who are appointed to direct the study
of them in our theological schools. It is a
question which, whatever we may think of the
occasion or the methods which have preci-
pitated it upon us, has been pushed to the
front by tendencies and conditions the operation of which it was not within the power
of man to stem or to control.   Now that
the issue is upon us we must meet it, in no
temper of suspicion, prejudice, or partisanship,
but in a frank, manly, straightforward way,
and in a spirit of loyalty to the truth, to
our Church, and to God. As to the personal
form which the issue has taken, as a movement to challenge and to invoke the formal

and authoritative condemnation, by the Presbyterian Church of the United States of America, of certain utterances respecting the Scriptures, and Scripture truths, recently made by a prominent theological professor in our Church, I shall have very little directly to say. I am not concerned to justify the utterances of my brother professor in detail. In that particular, my friend is abundantly able to take care of himself. If, as I confidently hope, the views which are here urged shall obtain from the Church, in its ultimate decision, the recognition which is claimed for them as scriptural, evangelical, confessional, scientific, reverent, and indispensable to the satisfactory and permanent solution of the great problems of our age, and to the harmony of religious faith with scientific and critical processes and results, I have no fear that any one will be wronged. The principles which are at stake are to my mind more vital than any personal issue. The movement of which I have spoken, and the utterances in the press and elsewhere which have accompanied and interpreted its inception and purpose, convince me that the time has come for a definite understanding respecting the rights of Christian Scholarship in the Biblical departments of our Theological Seminaries. That is a question in which I may be pardoned for feeling an intense personal interest. It is a question which affects

my calling, my work, my very life. If there
is anything in which my whole being is
wrapped up, it is the study and teaching of
the Word of God. If there is anything that
I love with every fibre of every heart-string,
it is that blessed old Book. If there is anything for which, so far as I know myself, I
would gladly lay down my life, it is that
this Book may be known and read throughout the length and breadth of the world as
the guide of lost souls to heaven. It is
because I believe in this Book with a conviction and love which grow with every year's
study of it, that I take my present position.
And it is because I believe that, in order
the sooner and the better to accomplish its
mission in the world, it must be rescued out
of a false position, and be put before the world
where it puts itself, that I would fain help in
clearing off the stumbling-blocks which mistaken zeal has put in the way of inquiring
souls, and dig down through the quicksands
of false definitions and untenable theories to
what Mr. Gladstone so truly and forcibly calls,
" *The impregnable Rock of Holy Scripture.*"

As I have already said, the time has come
for a definite understanding in regard to what
I may briefly call the Biblical situation. What
have we the right to teach about the Bible ?
We must come to a clear and cordial understanding in respect to that question. I trust.

it is not vanity that prompts me to hope I may say something that will help to bring about such an understanding. I would fain believe that I am in a position to understand both sides of the question at issue. There is much in the position of the brethren whose course on the particular issue before us I feel constrained to oppose that commands my hearty assent. I honour, I hope I share in their zeal for the supreme authority of the Word of God. In their opposition to every movement of thought which tends to undermine that authority, I am with them. If I believed that the apprehensions which inspire their present action were well grounded, I would earnestly support it.

I furthermore believe that it is all-important that there should be the most thorough accord between the work that is done and the instruction that is given in our seminaries, and the work done and the instruction given in our pulpits and parishes. There should be the most hearty unity of thought, feeling, and action, between theological professors and pastors, in our common work for the Master. I believe it is incumbent on both sides to maintain this *entente cordiale.* It is incumbent on us as professors so to carry on our work that the hands of our brethren in the field shall be strengthened. We are under obligation to do nothing that we can con-

sistently avoid doing that will discourage, disturb, embarrass them in their great and holy
mission, and so to train the young men under
our care that they shall go forth equipped
to reinforce them at every point. On the
other hand, I claim from my brethren reci-
procity in this matter. I ask that they accord
to us their confidence, that they beware of
unjust suspicions, that they try to understand
us in our position and work.

Good old Dr. Johnson used to say, " Clear
your mind of cant." Let us try to clear our
minds of cant, of mist, of prejudice in respect
to the issue we are trying. I cannot help
the conviction that the trouble of the present
situation, the ferment, the unsettlement, the
alarm which prevails, is due very largely—I
will not say altogether, but largely—and I
must say mainly, to a vague and inadequate
conception of the situation, leading to a confusion of terms and ideas, and resulting in mistaking friends for foes. In Matthew Arnold's
words :

> And we are here as on a darkling plain,
> Swept with confused alarms of struggle and flight,
> Where ignorant armies clash by night.

There is a good deal of unprofitable mental
gymnastics going on, such as Paul was so
careful to avoid. Some of our good brethren,
I fear, are " beating the air," and quite a

number, I am sure, are beating the wrong man.

There is an uncomfortable lack of definiteness and precision in certain charges which are made. We are hearing much about " errors," " dangerous errors," " erroneous tendencies," matters which are "calculated to unsettle faith." What are these " errors "? I suspect, if our brethren who complain of these things should undertake to frame a declaration, after the model of the Auburn Declaration, setting forth in black and white, first in the light of Scripture, and then in the light of the Confession, on this side the Error, and over against it the True Doctrine, the case would begin to look very differently from what it does. At all events we should then know precisely where we are, and exactly what we are talking about. Differences often arise from ambiguities. We use the same word in different senses, or we convey the same thought by different phrases, and then appeal to the General Assembly, forsooth, to decide between us ! Then again the world is moving on, and it is getting more and more hard to keep up with it. We are living in an age of specialties, and of specialists. Even among experts, the ninety and nine know not what the hundredth man is up to. They know that they are liable any fine morning to wake up and to find the Babylon of their fine old-

fashioned theories blown up with the dynamite
of some experiment, and Number One Hundred
dancing on the ruins.

Now it so happens that, in the Providence
of God, for better or worse, my lot has been
cast in a Theological Seminary. It has been
a necessity of my position to give some attention to the leading Biblical questions of the
day. For a quarter of a century this has been
my business. I trust, therefore, it will not be
regarded as presumption on my part if I
indulge the hope that by something I may
say, I may succeed in bringing some of my
brethren into closer touch with the best Christian Scholarship of the day touching some of
the questions which are involved in the present
issue. All I claim for myself is that I think I
understand both sides; and sympathising as
I do with both sides in some things, I would
fain bring them nearer together. And if I
make a more liberal use of the first personal
pronoun than is generally deemed commendable, you will understand my motive.

Allow me, then, to premise that in the
study of Biblical questions, which my vocation
has made necessary, I have both striven to
keep an open mind, and earnestly sought the
guidance of a wisdom higher than my own.
My study of the history of the interpretation
and criticism of God's Word has shown me,
as clearly as it has taught me anything, that

God does lead His people onward in their inquiries of His holy Oracle. I know, as well as I know anything, that progress, wonderful progress, has been made in my own day in the knowledge of the Word. I do not claim that all movement has been progress, or that every "find" has been a gain. I am well aware that in Biblical science, as in every science, there are rash speculations, unproved hypotheses, wild and dangerous vagaries. Some corners of the field are full of will-o'-the-wisps, illusive, unsubstantial, unsafe, gleaming, I fear, with a light that is not from heaven.

But, on the other hand, there are conclusions in this field which all, whose judgment is worth anything, are agreed in regarding as substantially established. There are other conclusions which must fairly be conceded to have a strong balance of probability in their favour. These conclusions must be reckoned with. Whether we accept them, or reject them, the data on which they are based must be satisfactorily explained. There are certain ascertained facts—so far as any historical data can be called facts—bearing on the structure of the Bible, bearing on the historical accuracy of particular statements in the Book, bearing on the inspiration of Scripture — facts bearing, that is, on the mode in which the accuracy, the infallibility, the inspiration, the authority of Scripture must be conceived and defined—

which can not be set aside by sneers at the Higher Criticism, which can not be offset by vague denunciations of Rationalism, which can not be disposed of at all without satisfying the demands of the most enlightened reason, the requirements of the most thorough scholarship, as well as the claims of the devoutest faith. We must reckon with these facts. We must take them into account. We must assign them their true value. We must make them the basis of our judgments and our deliverances. If the theories of other days will not bear the pressure of these facts they must go to the wall. There is no help for it. If your definition of inspiration, your definition of the infallibility of the Bible—mark what I say! not the doctrine, but *your definition* of the doctrine—if that definition will not stand the test of the established results of criticism, if it will not harmonize with ascertained facts, then so much the worse for the definition.

Two years ago it was my privilege to attend the sessions of the Free Church Assembly in Edinburgh, when Dr. Dods was elected to the Chair of Exegetical Theology in the New College. The candidature of Dr. Dods was strenuously resisted on the ground of his utterances respecting the Scriptures and their inspiration. The attempt was made to prove the unsoundness of his views. How? From Scripture? No! From the Confession of Faith? Not at all;.

but from Dr. Hodge on the Confession. At
once, from all parts of the house, the cry was
heard : " Dr. Hodge is not the Confession."
That summed up the situation in Scotland.
That sums up the situation here to-day. The
Commentary is not the Confession ; the Confession, let me add, is not Scripture. But
Dr. Hodge is neither Confession nor Scripture.
Or to state the case more broadly : the Scholastic Theology, which Dr. Hodge represents,
is neither the Confession nor the Word of God.
But there are dearly beloved brethren, throughout the Presbyterian Church, who are labouring
under the delusion that, if Dr. Hodge is not the
Confession, at least it means, or ought to mean,
what Dr. Hodge says. I hope to show, before
I get through, that it does mean nothing of the
sort.

But what does Dr. Hodge say is the teaching of the Confession ? In brief this : The
books of Scripture " are one and all, in thought
and verbal expression, in substance and form,
wholly the Word of God, conveying with
absolute accuracy and Divine authority, all that
God meant them to convey, without human
additions or admixtures." " All written under
it [the Divine influence called inspiration] is
the very Word of God, of infallible truth and
of Divine authority ; and this infallibility and
authority attach as well to the verbal expression in which the revelation is conveyed as to

the matter of the revelation itself." * Or still more comprehensively and explicitly, in a joint article written by Drs. A. A. Hodge and B. B. Warfield, we are told : " The historical faith of the Church has always been that all the affirmations of Scripture of all kinds, whether of spiritual doctrine, or duty, or of physical or historical fact, or of psychological or philosophical principle, are without any error when the *ipsissima verba* of the original autographs are ascertained and interpreted in their natural and intended sense.†

That statement, I take it, gives us the key to the situation. It is the premise from which have proceeded all the movements in our Church which have been directed, during the past ten years, against the affirmations of modern Biblical Criticism. The critics have found that statement of inspiration impossible. Therefore their conclusions are denounced as dangerous, rationalistic, or worse. This, however, as I hope to demonstrate, is not the position of our Standards. On this point our Doctors of Divinity are not the Confession. But before coming to that point, I wish to say one or two other things about that statement.

And first I charge upon it that it is unscien-

---

* *Commentary on the Confession of Faith*, by Dr. A. A. Hodge, p. 55.

† *The Presbyterian Review*, Vol. II. p. 238.

tific. It is an abstract, *a priori* affirmation, not resting on objective facts, but evolved out of the depths of the dogmatic consciousness. The inductive study of the Word of God was practically unknown at the time when that definition was framed, three hundred years ago. It proceeds from certain postulates respecting what God *must do* in the matter of inspiration, which are assumed at the outset, without proof, with no adequate basis in the facts of the case, with no support from any positive declaration by God Himself. These postulates are the product of the Scholasticism of the Post-Reformation age, which had inherited the methods, and followed largely in the lines of the Romish Scholasticism of the Middle Ages. Undoubtedly there was incomparably more of the material of Bible truth in the Protestant than in the Romish Scholasticism —for our Schoolmen did read their Bibles, and study their Bibles, and got their theology out of their Bibles—and for the time it was in many ways a grand and mighty theology. But their method—and it is of that I am now speaking—was seriously defective. Such definitions as I have just presented could legitimately rest only on the most exhaustive induction of all the facts and phenomena relating to the revelation of God in His Word ; first collecting and collating these facts, then estimating, analysing, classifying them, and, lastly, generalising from them according to the most rigorous laws of the inductive process, omitting nothing, inventing nothing, assuming nothing, distorting nothing. Is that the case? Surely it would be a rash and unhistoric claim. The older scholastic theory, which formulated that theory, which has dominated our dogmatic definitions down to the present day, under the influence of which most of us have been trained, knew nothing of this inductive process, did nothing of it.

And now, let me ask, is that safe ground to take? Is it safe, in this inductive age, to base a scientific definition on unscientific premises, to reach a scientific result by unscientific processes, to expose the citadel of your position at a thousand points to the strategic attacks of the scientific method? Remember that weakness at any one of those points lets in the enemy. Is it safe to stake the authority of the Scriptures on the absolute infallibility of every one of a thousand particulars, every one of which is subject to the remorseless probings of a science which cares nothing for your theories, cares very little, possibly, for your beliefs, refuses to know any thing but facts? Is that safe when, *according to your theory*, the loss of one particular means the loss of all."* Even

---

* "A proved error in Scripture contradicts not only our doctrine, but the Scripture claims, and therefore its inspi-

Drs. Hodge and Warfield make this admission :
"There will undoubtedly be found upon the
surface [of Scripture] *many* apparent affirmations *presumably inconsistent* with the present
teachings of science, with facts of history, or
with other statements of the sacred books
themselves." Surely it is not inconceivable
that in a number of particulars, or say only in
one particular, that presumption of unscientific,
unhistoric, contradictory teaching may turn
out to be more than a presumption. Then
what becomes of your theory? What, on your
theory, becomes of the authority of Scripture?

But I have a still more serious charge to
bring against this *a priori* method in theology
when applied to inspiration. For inspiration
is a *Divine Process*. What this process is in
its interior nature we can never know. It is
God that inspires, as it is God that creates, and
we can no more say how God inspires than how
God creates. What are the necessary, interior,
Divine conditions of inspiration? What do we
know about that? What *can* we know about
that? All we can know about it must be
derived from the terms which describe it, the
characteristics which it exhibits, the concrete
result which it produces, the effects which
follow it. And so I charge further upon this

ration, in making those claims." Drs. Hodge and Warfield,
Presbyterian Review, Vol. II. p. 245.
    * *The Presbyterian Review*, Vol. II., p. 237.

a priori definition of inspiration, that it is not only unscientific, but irreverent, presumptuous, lacking in the humility with which we should approach a Divine Supernatural Fact. Of course, I do not mean to charge *conscious* irreverence or presumption on those who frame or hold this theory, but remembering that unconscious faults attach to the best of men, I believe that Charles Kingsley never said a truer or a finer thing than that " there is an intimate connection between the health of the moral faculties and that of the inductive ones ; " and that " God does in science as well as in ethics hide things from the wise and prudent, from the proud, complete, self-contained systematiser like Aristotle. . . . and reveals them to babes, to gentle, affectionate, simple-hearted men, such as we know Archimedes to have been, who do not try to give an explanation for a fact, but feel how awful and Divine it is, and wrestle reverently and steadfastly with it, as Jacob with the Angel, and will not let it go until it bless them."*

Now, I claim that to say beforehand that inspiration, or any such Divine process, must be this or that, that it must have certain characteristics, is to venture beyond our limits, to step in where angels fear to tread. You may ask, Is not all that God does perfect ?

* *Alexandria and Her Schools.* Lecture I.

Most assuredly. But who are we, to define
that perfection, to formulate its constituents,
to legislate its conditions, to decide beforehand
that it must be thus, that it cannot be so, that
this is indispensable, that impossible? We are
told that at the end of each creative Day God
looked on what He had done, "and saw that it
was good." And what does God mean by
"GOOD"? Absolute, abstract perfection in
every particular, flawless regularity in every
line and curve, faultless fitness in every limb
and joint, infallible inerrancy, no wandering
stars, no jostling bodies, music of the spheres,
without a jarring note? That is, no doubt,
what *a priori* speculation would have affirmed.
If our friend, the Dogmatist, had stepped upon
the scene in time, before telescope, or microscope, or spectroscope was known, that is
precisely what he would have laid down for us
as the only orthodox view. He would have
had his definition of perfection, turned out of
his machine, square, rigid, all the sides exactly
parallel, every angle ninety degrees down to the
infinitesimal, every line as straight as the
shortest possible distance between two points
could make it—an exquisite specimen of logical
carpentering. "Nothing else"—he would
have assured us, with that superb confidence
which would be so imposing if it had not so
often imposed on us—"nothing else is conceivable or possible in the premises ; nothing

else would be worthy of God. What God
calls good must be a perfect result, complete,
flawless, faultless, infallible in every detail."
But look at the record; what do you find?
Irregularities, breaks, misfits, broken joints,
deformities, mutilations, abortions, collisions,
discords, imperfections all the way along; and
God back of it all, God over it all, God through
it all, God in it all, pushing on His way,
working out His will, and accomplishing—
yes, a Perfect Result! Ah! brethren, God's
thoughts are not as our thoughts, His ways
are not as our ways. The designs by which
He works are not patterns for Patent Office
purposes, not pieces of dilettante china-decora-
tion, not æsthetic models in waxwork, "faultily
faultless, icily regular, splendidly null." No,
sirs! The Patterns of Deity are commensu-
rate with Himself, they spread over His
eternity, they lose themselves in His infinitude,
they are awful with the glories and glooms of
His unsearchable wisdom, they are rugged and
ragged and riven with the thunders and
lightnings of omnipotence; they sweep on—
a Flood of measureless, resistless might—from
the Beginning which has no beginning to the
End which has no end; and what seem to us
to be flaws or fractures, miscarriages and mis-
chances, are swallowed up and borne along in
the Infinite Tide of His Purpose, the flow of
which they no more arrest, or disturb, or

weaken, than the shattered foam-bells, or wavering reflows of the Rapids above the Horseshoe Falls affect the plunge of Niagara. Flaws? Yes; but look at the Plan, massive with the lines and the curves of the Infinite and the Eternal, stamped with the symmetries and the sublimities of a Divine Art, charged with the perfect purposes of the Will which never fails. Frictions? Yes; but look at the matchless correlations of energy, the actions and interactions of endlessly articulated forces, that determine the balancings of the dew-drops, and swing Jupiters and suns and systems along their vast and mighty courses. Discords? Yes; but listen to the Eternal Anthem, the *Jubilate Deo*, that rings from star to star, and ravishes the eternities.

If, now, in creation God can work out a perfect result through imperfection, why not in inspiration? But here—in inspiration—there is another factor to be taken into the account, to wit, the human factor. In the production of Scripture we are concerned with two co-efficients. It is not God working alone, but God working with human instrumentalities, and using these instrumentalities, not as dead, passive things, but as free, integral, independent personalities; not as a mechanic uses his tools, not as a magician handles his puppets, but as a Living Spirit, breathing in and through living souls.

Now, it is a law of the Divine Operation
that in working under finite conditions it
respects those conditions ; that in using created
and limited agencies, it has regard for the
limitations of those agencies. I am far from
saying that no more is accomplished than
would be accomplished if the agent were left
to itself. What I do hold is that *the more* in
the case, the supra-natural *plus, is* supernatural,
not natural. The process here, as we are all
agreed, is a supernatural process, the result is
a Divine supernatural result. So much is not
questioned. What now? Just this : While
fully recognising the Divine supernatural
co-efficient, the Divine supernatural process,
and the Divine supernatural result, we must
also recognise the lower, finite co-efficient as
continuing unalterably itself. Its qualities, its
possibilities, its activities, its inherent limitations remain the same. There is no change of
essence, of structure, of elemental potency.
An inanimate agent, when supernaturally commissioned, does not become animate. The
fire of a miracle is never anything but fire.
The *pneuma* of a dead wind is never changed,
as the Rabbis of old thought, into the *pneuma*
of a living spirit. The irrational brute is not
transformed into a rational being. The raven
that fed Elijah was nothing more than a bird.
Nor does man, when supernaturally influenced,
cease to be a man. An inspired man is not

God. Dr. Charles Hodge says, most truly and beautifully: "When He ordains praise out of the mouths of babes, they must speak as babes, or the whole power and beauty of the tribute will be lost."* Inspiration does not change the human personality, does not efface its inherent qualities, does not expunge its limitations, does not change the finite into the infinite, the human into the superhuman. That is the law, the universal law in nature and in history. If we engage in *à priori* speculation at all, it should be along the line of that law. Reasoning antecedently along that line, proceeding from *the actual* to the probable, basing our conclusions on what we see through all the works of God, we should *expect to find*, in the human co-efficient of a supernatural revelation, the inherent limitations of that co-efficient. So far are we from being entitled to say beforehand that God *must* make His human auxiliary superhumanly infallible in every possible particular, that the very opposite is alone what analogy justifies us in affirming.

Brethren, let me give another illustration of the danger of such *à priori* speculation concerning what God must be or do in the revelation of Himself; and may God help me to treat the subject with all becoming reverence. The Mystery of mysteries in God's

* *Systematic Theology.* Vol. I., page 157.

revelation of Himself to men is the Incarnation. " In the beginning was the Word, and the Word was with God, and the Word was God, . . . and the Word became flesh." That such a thing would be, that such a thing *could* be, is what no human speculation could have anticipated, what no human intellect could have deemed possible. But let me suppose that in some way, by some sweet, Divine intimation, the thought had come to some devout mind, as, for aught we know, it may have come to one or another, that one day God would become man. How would he have conceived it ? How from his narrow premises must he have conceived it ? Is it not natural to suppose that he would have formulated his conception something after this fashion : " Will God indeed come down and dwell among men as one of them ? What an august spectacle will that be ! What a transcendent type of manhood in all respects will the world then witness ! What perfection ! What dignity ! What invincible strength ! What unapproachable, awe-inspiring majesty ! How immeasureably exalted above all His human fellows will that being be ! How serenely impervious to all the disturbances and distractions of the weltering moral chaos around Him ! How Divinely exempt from all the weaknesses, the imperfections, the stumblings and strivings of the wretched

weaklings to whom He had descended! God
a man! How can I believe it? But if a man,
then surely man at his best!" A natural
expectation, would it not be? Would the
opposite picture have been anticipated, have
been deemed probable, or even possible?
What! an Incarnate God down in the dregs
of human existence! passing through, sharing
in the infantile dependence, weakness, ignorance, discipline, growth of a creature! coming
up like a root out of dry ground, with no
beauty or comeliness, that men should desire
Him! bowed to the earth with a burden of
unutterable shame and anguish! and sweating
great drops of blood in the throes of the
conflict! trembling with fear and praying
with strong cryings for delivery! touched with
the feeling of our infirmities! helped by an
angel! tried in all things like as we are!
learning—yes, learning—obedience by His
sufferings! tempted! baffled! groaning!
weeping! agonising! forsaken of the Father!
Man's feeble logic could never have grasped
this tremendous mystery.* It could never

---

* It is enough to refer to the Messianic hopes of the
Jewish people, their rejection of Chist because His coming
was so opposed to all their preconceptions, and to the
painful slowness with which even the disciples became
reconciled to the reality. How instructive are Peter's
remonstrances and Christ's rebuke, as recorded in Matt. xvi.
21-23.

have dreamed it. It would have protested
against it. It must have pronounced it
impossible. If, then, it would have been a
mistake, nay, as we now see, a mistake bor-
dering on blasphemy (see Matt. xvi. 23) to
pronounce antecedently against an incarnate
revelation of God, subject to the limitations of
weakness, of ignorance, of bondage, to the
contractions and detractions of that ineffable
Kenosis of the Godhead, ought we not to be
most reverently slow, most cautious, most
humble, in pronouncing against an inspired
revelation of God, subject to certain wisely
permitted limitations of human weakness,
ignorance and fallibility?* What know we
of the Divine Thought? How know we what
Divine, infallible, and perfect Purpose may be
served even by these limitations and falli-
bilities? Does not Scripture itself intimate
that at least there *is* such a purpose, and that
it does work through just such channels of
human frailty? Is not God's strength always
made perfect in man's weakness? Has not
God committed His treasures to earthen
vessels, that the exceeding greatness of the
power may be of God? Did not God choose
"the foolish things of the world, that He
might put to shame them that are wise; the
weak things of the world that He might put

* See the extract from Mr. Gladstone further on.

to shame the things that are strong; and the base things of the world, and the things that are despised, . . . yea, and the things that are not, that He might bring to naught the things that are?" If God thus chooses to work out His problems through surds and fractions and zeros, who are we to say Him nay? Brethren, this is God's way; this is the law. What right have we to say where that law shall stop? to decide how much of the earthen vessel shall count as a factor? how much or how little of the human folly, weakness, nothingness, is compatible with the Divine Purpose? God is not limited as to His means and methods in communicating His will to men. Had a literal, stereotyped, incorruptible infallibility in every jot and tittle of the record been an indispensable requisite, God had a thousand resources at His command for securing such a record. That He chose men, yes, men with all their ignorance, and weakness and fallibility; that He intrusted His revelation to their stammering tongues and to their stumbling pens; that He deposited the interpretation of His eternal ways in earthen vessels, which could not escape the corruptions and mutilations of time; simply shows that a literal, particularistic infallibility is of less moment in the sight of God than some other things; of less worth, perhaps, than the thrill of a human touch, the glow of a red-hot word, the pulse of a throbbing heart, the lightning of a living eye, the flash of a soul on fire ; of less worth—who knows ?—than the faltering of the pilgrim's foot, dearer to heaven than the lordly step of Gabriel. If I rightly interpret Paul in the tenth chapter of Romans, and elsewhere, it is one chief glory of the Gospel as compared with the Law that it is not a formal, stereotyped letter, but a personal voice, a living heart, a breathing soul, the effluence of a divinely magnetized personality, an epistle written not with ink, but with the Spirit of the living God.* Calvin E. Stowe was not far from right when he said : " It is not the words of the Bible that were inspired. It is not the thoughts of the Bible that were inspired. It is the men who wrote the Bible that were inspired." † I feel constrained, accordingly, to protest against the *a priori* assumption that God can not or will not inspire men wthout making them infallible as Himself, as unscientific, against all analogy, irreverent, and

---

* See'Rom. x. : 8-10, 14-18 ; xii. : 1 f., 5 f. ; 1 Cor. i. : 4 f.,. 17 f. (21) ; ii. : 1 f. ; iii. : 9 f. ; ix. : 2 ; xii. : 4 f. (12, 13, 27) ; 2 Cor. ii. : 14 ; iii. : 2 f. ; iv. : 6 f. (13) ; vi. : 1 f. ; Gal. 1. : 15, 16 ; Eph. i. : 17 f. (19, 23) ; ii. : 10, iii. : 20, 21 ; v. : 7 f. ; Phil. i. : 7, 20, 27 f. ; ii. : 15 f. ; Col. i. : 3 f. (6), 9 f. ; ii. : 6 f. ; iv. : 5 ; 1 Thes. i. : 8 ; ii. : 12, 13 ; 2 Thes. i. : 3 f., 11 f. Cf. 1 Pet. ii. : 5 f., 9 f., 11 f., 15 f. ; iii. : 1 f., 15 f. ; iv. : 10 f.

† *History of Books of the Bible,* p. 19.

presumptuous, as well as unscriptural and con-
tradicted by the facts.

In all humility, therefore, instead of dictating
what God must do, let us inquire reverently
what God has done, how God has spoken; in
what form, really, actually, concretely, practically, the revelation of His will has come to
men. It is a theme on which volumes might
be written. I can at this time only single out
a few salient points. And as my own particular field of study is the New Testament, I
will limit the present discussion to that field.
There is this advantage, also, in looking at this
department of the subject: that if the theory
I am opposing is valid anywhere, it applies
to the New Testament; if it breaks down
there it will hold nowhere.

I must call attention at the outset to the
disadvantage under which the defence even of
the best attested conclusions of modern criticism labours from the serious lack of acquaint-
ance with these conclusions which the attacks
made upon them generally betray. Most of
the discussions which have come under my
notice in our religious journals and elsewhere
evince a quite inadequate appreciation of the
present situation as touching Biblical Science.
As against the conclusions of to-day, they are
for the most part as ineffectual as the guns of
1860 would be against an ironclad ship or fort
of 1890. These three decades have effected an

enormous change, a revolution, in fact, in the problems to be solved, in the difficulties to be removed, in the positions to be assumed in the defence of the truth.

Let me give one illustration : These thirty years have witnessed the birth and early growth of one new and most important branch of Biblical Science. I refer to Biblical Theology, the very chair out of which the utterances have proceeded which have occasioned the present agitation. Thirty years ago that science, as it is understood and prosecuted to-day, was unknown. It is a young discipline, as yet, with much work before it, but entering vigorously on its career, blazing its way, proceeding on lines of its own, working by methods of its own, and elaborating results which have their distinct place and value in the science of the Bible. Young as it is, it has already accomplished marvels. It has opened up new vistas of thought, established new starting-points of inquiry. It has propounded, and is daily propounding new questions to solve. It is necessitating new solutions of old questions. It is bringing old facts into new foci, as well as bringing new facts to light. It is putting old truths under new lights, and if not discovering new truths, it is at least compelling new and larger statements of the old eternal verities. Its conclusions cannot fail to have a most important and decisive bearing on the religious and theological thought of the future. And yet I have seen in our religious journals articles and paragraphs criticising, and even resenting, the claims put forth in behalf of Biblical Theology, as though the advocates of that science were advertising some special patent of their own, or vaunting some special quality of their personal theology, to the disparagement of every other. The same sort of objection, proceeding from the same want of familiarity with the subject, has often been urged against the " Higher Criticism," as though it arrogated for itself a higher level than your criticism or mine. Those whom I am now addressing have seen and heard such complaints respecting these sciences. They have seen it argued not so very long ago that the champions of Biblical Theology were arrogating quite too much for their favourite study ; that all sound theology is Biblical Theology, Hodge's Theology, Shedd's Theology, and the rest. But can this sort of thing be accepted as competent criticism ? Systematic Theology and Biblical Theology are distinct disciplines, as much so as Logic and Mathematics. Mathematics may be logical, but Mathematics are not Logic. Systematic Theology may be biblical, but it is not Biblical Theology. I beg your pardon for dealing in such truisms ; I only regret that it seems to be necessary. Biblical Theology was hardly in its cradle when Dr. Charles Hodge wrote his three

volumes of Systematic Theology, and I know of
no dogmatic system that can be said to exhibit
any distinct consciousness or trace of the influence of the sister science. The methods of the
two are in fact well-nigh incompatible. Dogmatic Theology is largely deductive ; Biblical
Theology inductive. The former aims to be
systematic and logical ; the latter critical and
exegetical. The one deals with revealed truth
chiefly in its abstract forms ; the other in its
concrete, historic, and personal expressions.*
Systematic Theology lumps all the books of
the Bible together, arranges their miscellaneous contents around some philosophic centre,
or along certain logical lines, picking out one
passage here, another passage there, as the
exigency on the one side, and the fitness on
the other seem to justify ; disregarding, or at
most regarding only in a very meagre way, the
different connections, the variant types, the
remote and often antithetic points of view,
the gradual evolutions, the higher and lower
planes of thought and belief. Biblical Theology
studies the Bible as Astronomy studies the
heavens ; each star or planet—Sirius, Mars,
Mercury, Venus—in its own place, orbit, life,

---

* See *Reuss's History of Christian Theology in the
Apostolic Age,* Introduction, Chap. I., " Scholastic and
Biblical Theology." *Weiss's Biblical Theology of the
New Testament,* Introduction, § 1, " The Problem of the
Science."

development, movement, the minor systems,
Jupiter and Saturn, with their moons, the con-
stellations, asteroids, nebulæ, and all that tells
the story of the heavens. So Biblical Theology
looks at and inquires into each separate star,
the prophetic and apostolic clusters, the major
and minor systems, the binaries, asteroids,
satellites, and star-dust, uttering meanwhile
the prayer of the saintly Herbert :

> Oh, that I knew how all thy lights combine,
>   And the configuration of their glorie !
> Seeing not only how each verse doth shine,
>   But all the constellations of the storie.

Dogmatic Theology subjects Scripture to
the logical categories, the metaphysical termi-
nology, the polemic accentuations, the ecclesiastical dogmas, which eighteen centuries of
uninspired reflection and speculation on the
contents of Scripture have imposed on our
interpretation of the same. Biblical Theology
takes us direct to the fountain-head, to the
original material as it is in itself, as it lies
in its providential environment, as it gushes
out of the living well-spring, as by the Divine
ordering of time and place and person it pours
its living contribution into the great River of
Life.

The theology of the schools is based on
the principle of systematic self-consistency.
It is a logical unit ; and by an instinct of self-

preservation it ignores it if it can, it excludes
as far as it can, or if it must recognise, it
belittles and attenuates all it can the antithetic truths which would imperil the unity
of the system. The Arminian dogmatism does
this with the Calvinistic side of the Gospel.
The Calvinistic dogmatism does the same with
the Arminian side. One *Dogmatik* says: "I am
of Cephas." It fails of absorbing the best part
of Peter, and leaves out Apollos altogether.
Another says: "I am of Paul." It excludes
John, and leaves out one whole side of Paul,
absorbing his particularism, perchance, but
failing to assimilate his universalism. But
the Theology of the Book and of its books
is weighted with no such logical embarrass-
ments. It aims to ascertain what *every* inspired teacher has to say, and *all* that each
inspired teacher says, *all* of Peter, *all* of John,
all of James, *all* of Paul, their antinomies,
their ἅπαξ λεγόμενα, and their ἅπαξ νοούμενα,
their polarities and their paradoxes, their pro-
vincialisms, as also their large spiritual
cosmopolitanisms.

It is not strange that the conclusions of
Biblical Theology should at times seem sus-
picious to those who have read their Bibles
only through the glasses of one-sided dogmatism. There are more things in the heaven
and earth of the younger science than have
been dreamed of in the philosophy of the other.

There are aspects of Redemption, of which Paul, for example, is full, a race-redemption,* cosmic reconciliation,† the re-unification of the universe,‡ of which your scholastic theology knows little or nothing.   Dogmatism gives us one phase of santification, as we find it predominantly perhaps in Paul, as a subjective, progressive process, predicated of the Christian in this life.   But what of other statements in Paul, such as that, " He who began a good work in you will perfect it until the day of Jesus Christ "? §   What of the objective sanctification of the Epistle to the Hebrews ? What of " the purification of heaven " itself in that Epistle ?   What of the objective-subjective sanctification of the Apostle John, in which there is no recognition of progress even in this life, but which is presented as a single absolute fact?   If now, by the study of Biblical Theology, I have been aided to the better appreciation of these many-sided representations of Divine Truth, am I to be shut up to the one-sided interpretation of a theology to which this method of studying

---

* 1 Rom. v. 8; xi. 32; xv.; 8 f.; 1 Cor. xv. 22; 2 Cor. v 15; 1 Tim. iv. 10; Tit. ii. 11.   And cf. Gal. iii. 8; Phil. ii. 10; 1 Tim. ii. 4—6.

† Rom. xi. 15 (cf. v. 12) ; 2 Cor. v. 19.

‡ Eph. i. 10, 21—23; iv. 10; 1 Cor. xv. 24—28; 2 Cor. v. 17 f.; Phil. iii. 21 ; Col. i. 20.

§ Phil. i. 9; cf. 1 Cor. i. 8.

the Word was unknown? Is *all* of Divine Truth in our Systematic Theology? Is it *all* in the Confession of Faith? While going with these helps as far as they take us, are we never to go a step further?

Biblical Theology is of special importance in thus unfolding to us the compositeness of Bible truth, and in giving us the key to its rich and suggestive variations.* It puts us moreover in touch with *the man* who speaks to us in the name of God. We feel that in Peter, in John, in James, we have an inspired man, not a divinely-manipulated automaton. We come to understand why, in discussing the same subject, Paul says this, and says it thus ; James says that, and says it so ; why the first Evangelist gives this report of our Lord's discourses, the fourth Evangelist that report ; why the second Gospel puts such a fact in this light, the third Gospel in another. This *Novum Organum* of Biblical Theology, calling to its aid Criticism, the Higher and the Lower, puts us in possession of the human personal equation in the Inspired Word, as we never

* See especially Weiss, *Biblical Theology of the New Testament*, Introduction, § 1 (c). See also the excellent remarks which follow, (d), showing how a complete Scriptural systematic theology must build on this composite basis, uniting all the variations in a larger synthesis, which shall so far as possible harmonise all, without suppressing any.

possessed it before. It reveals to us what Farrar calls " The Messages of the Books"; nay more, the mission of each writer, known and unknown ; and helps us to see how even in his idiosyncracies, even in his limitations, each is fitted for his particular place and task. Take the Apostle Jude, for example. Look at him as illuminated by Biblico-Theological lights. What an interesting picture ! What a vivid personality ! With his intense Hebraism, his prophetic fire, his weird imagination, his antique eloquence, the apocalyptic tinge of his representation, his mental limitations even, his inability to get entirely outside the literary environment in which his mind has always moved, with its legendary exegesis and its apocryphal ingredients —but what of that? What is a cobweb on the mane of a lion? What is a fleck of soot, a speck of unassimilated carbon, hovering around the beacon-fire which warns the ship at sea off the rocks? What is a touch of mediævalism in Dante's Divine Comedy, or an anachronism in Milton's " Paradise Lost "? What if one or two minor details in Jude are to be estimated in the light of the man's literary environment, and qualified by the clearer teaching of the larger Word? Was he any the less a prophet and an apostle? Did not the Divine Light irradiate even these minute opaquer spots? Nay, did not even the relative crudity, which a more advanced New Testament Christianity soon left behind, have its own peculiar value and force for the time being, and for those whom he was specially addressing, and even by virtue of its being no more and no other than it was?

In this connection let me note very briefly the vast gain which has accrued to the critical faculty itself by the use of the improved critical methods of the present; the deeper insight, the increased delicacy and tact, the more facile apprehension of clues and their leadings, the finer appreciation of habits and drifts of thought, of undertones of sentiment and experience, of the modulations of mood and passion, of the *nuances* of phrasing and expression, of colour, atmosphere, tone, grouping, treatment;—the culture, in short, of those literary instincts and methods, the possession of which makes our age, however deficient in creative power, pre-eminent in critical skill. That there has been a palpable gain within the last half century in the application of expert tests to the criticism of the Bible on the literary side, no competent and fair-minded judge will deny.

But I pass on to consider more specifically the results obtained by the application of these tests to the Gospel record in the New Testament, and the significance of these results for our conception of the inspiration of that record. After a century of exhaustive investigation and sharp discussion, the most sober-minded and trustworthy critics are now rapidly reaching a consensus of judgment on this most important and vital subject. Certain conclusions may be regarded as established to the point of the highest reasonable probability. I will try to formulate these as briefly as possible, in so far as they are vital to the decision of the question before us. Beginning with the Synoptic Gospels,* it is now generally admitted that in the form in which we have them, they are derived immediately from certain written sources. These are mainly two : (1) A Fact—Source, consisting chiefly of deeds, incidents in the life of our Lord, together with such conversational or other remarks as naturally accompany them, to which may be added a few short discourses, parables, and the like. In its purest form this Source is identified with the principal groundwork of our Mark. It is found also as the pragmatic groundwork of Matthew and Luke. (2) A Word—or Logia—Source, consisting mainly, though not exclusively, of sayings and discourses of Christ,

* The limits of the occasion for which the paper was prepared prevented the carrying out of my original purpose to compare the Synoptic form of the Gospel with the Johannean. Those who are familiar with the most decisive conclusions of criticism on this head are well aware how greatly they would have strengthened the argument.

which we find in its earliest and most historic form in Luke, but in its fullest and most elaborate form in our Matthew, to whom the earliest tradition (represented by Papias) accredits it. The primary material of these Sources is unmistakably Apostolic, using the word in its broader New Testament sense.* It proceeds from credible eye-witnesses and inspired servants of the Word. This is directly asserted by Luke (i. 1 f.) and confirmed throughout by the internal characteristics of all the Gospel narratives.

This Double-Source Theory is now all but universally regarded as the key to the solution of the Synoptic problem.†

In addition to these two main Sources, there are other special documents peculiar to

* For which consult Bp. Lightfoot's Excursus on "The Name and Office of an Apostle," in his *Commentary on Galatians.*

† There is still room as yet for differences of opinion respecting the precise relations to each other of the original groundworks and present canonical forms of the Gospels. These differences do not affect, however, the more essential points in respect to which substantial unanimity prevails. See Prof. Bruce on "The Increasing Consensus Among Critics of All Schools and Countries," and on the way in which "the question is being gradually narrowed," *The Presbyterian Review*, Vol. V., p. 630. And compare Prof. Sanday's article, "A Survey of the Synoptic Question," in *The Expositor* of February, 1891, p. 87 f., and especially his Second Article in the March number, entitled "Points Proved or Probable," p. 179 f.

each Evangelist, notably Luke, as examples of which we may take the opening chapters respecting our Lord's birth and childhood, and ch. xv., with its immortal triad of parables.

These documentary sources, particularly the first two, were called forth by the inadequacy of the primitive oral tradition, for either the perpetuation or the dissemination of the Gospel record. They came to be of especial service in the instruction of catechumens ; and perhaps the most satisfactory explanation of the definiteness, uniformity, and universality, which they acquired, and which made it possible for them to supersede all other like documents of that age, is to be found in the catechumenical use that was made of them.*

---

* The proem of Luke's Gospel will be found especially instructive at this point. It will be noted that Luke recognised the twofold source of the record mentioned above. He accurately describes the former when he says that "Many have taken in hand to draw up a narrative concerning *the facts*" (περὶ τῶν πραγμάτων), as transmitted from the original "*eye-witnesses*" (οἱ ἀπ' ἀρχῆς αὐτόπται). He well describes the latter when he states his own object to be that Theophilus "might know the certainty of *the words* wherein he was catechetically instructed" (περὶ ὧν κατηχήθης λόγων). This last clause is also significant as to the catechetical function of the earlier Gospel records. Let it be noted, furthermore, that Luke's statement as to the primary sources of the material of these documentary records stamps them with the authority of credible and inspired witnesses. Ch. i., 2.

Looking at the way in which the Synoptic Evangelists have made use of these documents, we find that the versions to which they had access respectively, while substantially identical, must have varied in some details. There is internal evidence also that each adjusted and edited the material in his own way. Mark, *e.g.*, has stamped the groundwork of his Gospel with many vivid touches which may be distinctly traced to the personality of Peter. There are visible indications of Luke's own hand touching up the record in his Gospel, not seldom producing a marked variation from the more original type as exhibited in Matthew or Mark. He has a way, also, of supplying a " motive " for an incident or a parable, which is lacking in the other Evangelists, and which, however it be explained, at least increases the perplexity of the harmoniser. Matthew has a way of elaborating a particular discourse, or of grouping parables or facts, on other than strict historic lines. The Sermon on the Mount, *e.g.*, *as found in Matthew*, can not be regarded as a verbatim report of a single connected discourse, but rather as in the beginning, indeed, a memorable discourse, the historic form of which has been more clearly reproduced by Luke, which Matthew has enlarged by the addition of cognate remarks made at other times and places, and systematised into a more complete ideal presentation by Christ of the

principles and laws of His kingdom.   So also
in the report of our Lord's eschatological discourse, Matthew has, by the introduction of a
single word, " *immediately* after the tribulation
of those days" (xxiv. 29), foreshortened, in a
material way, the perspective of the whole
prophecy, putting Christ's final coming, in
accordance with the expectation of the Apostolic age, in the immediate future.*   Thus it
will be seen that the editorial elaboration and
adaptation of the source-material has tended in
the aggregate result to multiply and intensify
the individual peculiarities and divergencies of
the Synoptics rather than to bring them into
closer correspondence.

But back of these documentary sources lies
the oral traditional Gospel, the first form which
the Gospel record necessarily assumed, which,
of course, disappeared with the first generation
of Palestinian Christians, and soon passed over
into the written documentary form.   The
theory that our Gospel record was the direct
transcription of this oral Gospel, which was
for a time quite prevalent, has now been
abandoned by all the leading critics as inadequate to account for the facts, although it is

---

* Whether, as in the text, the insertion of ἐυθέως be
attributed to the editorial elaboration of Matthew, or its
omission to the editing of Mark and Luke, the effect in
either case on the prophetic perspective can not be
ignored.

not denied that there are features of the record for which the recognition of its influence would still help to account.*

Once more : Back of all these sources, oral and written, lies the important fact, now un-questioned, that our Lord's discourses were spoken in Aramaic, and that to this language must be referred the great bulk of the original material of our Gospels. The first form of the oral Gospel was undoubtedly Aramaic. The first form of the Logia Source was, according to the express testimony of Papias, Aramaic. The basis of the other main Source was Aramaic, as we may reasonably infer from the study of Mark, its purest representative. The same was true, doubtless, of most of the other special documents, *e.g.* those of Luke, to which reference has been made.†

This is the account which the best modern criticism gives of the composition of the Syn-

* It should be noted that a single direct oral prototype of our written Gospel record is forbidden by the fact that already the New Testament record reflects three types of the tradition—to wit : the Marco-Petrine, the Matthaean (*Logia*), and the Johannean, leaving out of the account the indefinite floating mass of *Agrapha*, the study of which has at last been initiated by the recent work of Resch.

† On this feature of the case see the very interesting series of articles by Prof. Marshall, now publishing in *The Expositor*, on "The Aramaic Gospel."

optic Gospels. How does this account bear
on the interpretation of the record, and
on our conception of the mode of inspiration?

First, let us note that we have here the complex result of a complex process. Our study
of the Gospels, and especially of " the Harmony
of the Gospels," has made each one familiar
with the lack of perfect correspondence between the Gospel narratives. The Synoptic
story, I need not say, is full of breaks, leaps,
omissions here, additions there, transpositions
all the way along,* with many variations in
matters of detail, which by no means affect
the substance of the record, but which are an
endless and often insoluble perplexity to those
who are in search of an exact literal harmony ;
Osiander, *e.g.*, one of the earliest of our rigid
modern harmonists, finding it necessary, in
order to maintain the perfect consistency of
the record, to introduce Peter's wife's mother
as three times falling ill of a fever, of which
Christ three times healed her. We are all
familiar with these characteristics. But the
point I would emphasize is this : the prevalent

---

* " The Gospels, and especially the first three, can in no
sense be regarded as methodical annals. It is, therefore,
difficult, and perhaps impossible, so to harmonise them in
respect to time as in all cases to arrive at results which
shall be entirely certain and satisfactory."—Robinson's
Harmony of the Four Gospels in Greek: Introduction to
the Notes.

critical view of the structure of the Gospel
record puts a totally new aspect on the problem
of solving the irregularities and discrepancies.
So long as it was held that the "original autograph" of each Gospel was throughout the
original production of the author whose name
it bears ; that Matthew wrote out all the Gospel
under his name, as Plutarch, *e.g.*, wrote out
each of his Lives ; 'that Mark did the same
either from information supplied by Peter, or
by simply condensing Matthew ; that Luke at
least wrote out an original recast of Matthew
and Mark, with additions from sources of his
own—for this was substantially the old theory ;
it might perhaps be urged, with a show of
reason, that these differences, being known to
the authors, were intentional and susceptible
of an explanation to their minds, if not to
ours ; * that they were in large measure only a
question of order, of expansion, of condensa-
tion, of supplementation. Even then it was a
serious task to reconcile these divergencies in
such a way as to meet the requirements of

---

* "Such apparent inconsistencies and collisions with
other sources of information are to be expected in imper·
fect copies of ancient writings; from the fact that the
original reading may have been lost, or that we may fail to
realise the point of view of the author, or that we are
destitute of the circumstantial knowledge which would
fill up and harmonise the record."—Drs. Hodge and Warfield : *Presbyterian Review*, Vol. II., p. 237.

a verbal inspiration.* With the present conclusions of criticism, however, such an explanation is utterly out of the question. A re-
course to the *ipsissima verba* of the original
autograph fails us out and out. For the great
bulk of the Gospel material there is no original
autograph. There never was one. There was
no *ipsissima verba* report of our Lord's words
taken down on the spot. They passed into the
memory of those who heard them, and that in
their Aramaic form. The two basal records,
the Fact record, and the Word record, were
gradually organised out of those memories.
What of the *ipsissima verba* in that organising
process? † With the increasing demand for

---

* It may be well to state here, once for all, that in this
paper the expression "verbal inspiration" is in such connections as the above used for brevity, according to a
common usage, to designate the dogma of absolute verbal
inerrancy. It will be seen further along that I myself
hold strongly to the theopneustic quality of the words as
well as thoughts of Scripture.

† To relegate this traditional stage of the Gospel record
to the category of "Revelation," and to limit "Inspiration" to the written formulation, would be the height of
logical fatuity and self-contradiction. If an *ipsissima verba*
inspiration was needed anywhere, it surely was needed in
laying the foundations of the record. It was the consciousness of this, doubtless, which led Drs. Hodge and Warfield
to contradict their own logic and sharp discriminations by
saying of the superintendence which they identify with
the essence of inspiration that it "attended the entire
process of the genesis of Scripture."—*See Note* 2, p. 148.

exactness, perpetuity, and a wider circulation, the record gradually took the written form. How about the *ipsissima verba* in that process ? How close the correspondence between the oral and the written forms ? Who knows ? What modifications may have taken place ?—Who knows ? Soon came the need for a Greek record. Gradually the primary Aramaic material took on a secondary Greek form. How about the *ipsissima verba* in that process ? Did absolutely no modification take place ? How do we know that ? What changes may have come into the collation, the combination, the didactic and catechetical adaptation, the dissemination of the various numerous records ?* We know nothing of all this. We only know that without a standing *ipsissima verba* miracle running through every step of all these processes, an *ipsissima verba* result would have been impossible. What right have we to affirm that such a miracle was wrought? Where is the evidence ? Nay ! every advance which criticism has made in the examination of the Gospel record has only made it more and more certain that the varying representations of the record can be accounted for only as being the inevitable accompaniments of human fallibility in the complex processes through which the record reached its final form. It is now as certain as anything can

* Compare Luke i. 1.

well be, as a matter of historical record, that, when one Evangelist says that two blind men were healed by Christ near Jericho, while another mentions but one; when one describes the healing as taking place on the way into Jericho, the other on the way out; these variations are to be taken at their face value, as representing diversities in the sources, as the honest, but immaterial contradictions of honest human testimony, when subjected to the complicated and trying conditions through which the Gospel witness has passed—divergences which, so far from discrediting the essential fact, the miracle, only corroborate it to every candid judgment.*

But it is claimed that inspiration is not necessarily concerned with this process of building up the record, but with the final formulation of it.† I hope to show further along

---

* The same remark applies to the divergences found in the narratives of the healing of the centurion's servant (Matt. viii. 5 f.; Luke vii. 1 f.), and of the demoniac of Gadara (Matt. viii. 28 f.; Mark v. 1 f.; Luke viii. 26 f.); the calling of the Capernaum Apostles (Matt. iv. 18 f.; Mark i.; 16 f.; Luke v. 1 f.); the raising of Jairus's daughter (Matt. ix. 18 f.; Mark v. 22. f; Luke viii. 41 f.).

† "*In many cases* these gifts [Revelation and Inspiration] *were separated. Many of the sacred writers*, although inspired, received *no revelations.* This was probably the fact with the historical books of the Old Testament. The Evangelist Luke does not refer his knowledge of the events which he records to revelation, but says he derived it from those 'which from the beginning were eye-witnesses and mini-

what an utterly inadequate and unscriptural view of inspiration this gives us. For the pre-

sters of the Word.' *It is immaterial to us where* Moses obtained his knowledge of the events recorded in the Book of Genesis; whether *from early documents, from tradition,* or from direct revelation. No more causes are to be assumed for any effect than are necessary. If the sacred writers had sufficient sources of knowledge in themselves, *or in those about them,* there is *no need* to assume any direct revelation. It is enough for us that *they were rendered infallible as teachers.*"—Dr. Charles Hodge, *Systematic Theology,* Vol. 1., p. 155. " Inspiration is that Divine influence which, accompanying the sacred writers equally in all they wrote, secured the infallible truth of their writings in every part, both in idea and expression, and *determined the selection and distribution of their material* according to the Divine purpose." [Observe that nothing is said of the inspiration of the material. That is not assumed as necessary.] By what some writers, as Doddridge, Lee, &c., have called "the inspiration of *superintendence,*" is "meant *precisely* what we [Dr. A. A. Hodge] have given above *as the definition of inspiration.*"—Dr. A. A. Hodge, *Outlines of Theology,* pp. 67, 69. Drs. A. A. Hodge and B. B. Warfield, in their joint article, "*distinguish sharply* between Revelation, which is the *frequent* [but not constant], and Inspiration, which is the *constant* attribute of all the thoughts and statements of Scripture, and *between the problem of the genesis of Scripture* on the one hand, which includes historic processes and the concurrence of natural and supernatural forces, and must account for all the phenomena of Scripture; and *the* MERE FACT OF INSPIRATION on the other hand, *or the superintendence by God* of the writers *in the entire process of their writing,* WHICH ACCOUNTS FOR NOTHING WHATEVER BUT THE ABSOLUTE INFALLIBILITY *of the record in which the revelation, once generated, appears in* THE ORIGINAL AUTOGRAPH. It will be observed that we intentionally avoid applying to this

sent I am concerned with the literary and critical aspect of the position.

Note, to begin with, how strange it is that if an *ipsissima verba* infallibility, secured by a supervision which is the essence of inspiration, was essential, the record as it stands should present so many difficulties on that theory. We have heard of prohibition which does not prohibit, of protection which does not protect. Have we here an infallible supervisory inspiration which does not inspire infallibility? It looks very much like it, if we are shut up to the *ipsissima verba* theory.

Mark, again, that the difficulties which

---

inspiration the predicate 'influence.' It summoned on occasion a great variety of influences, *but its essence was superintendence.* This superintendence attended the entire process of the genesis of Scripture, *and particularly the process of* THE FINAL COMPOSITION OF THE RECORD."—*The Presbyterian Review*, vol. ii., p. 225 f. I cannot resist the temptation to call attention to the extraordinary logical confusion into which our *par nobile fratrum dogmaticorum* plunge in the last sentence. After "*distinguishing sharply*" between "*the genesis* of Scripture, and the mere fact of inspiration," or its equivalent and "essence"—to wit, "superintendence"—we are gravely assured that "*this superintendence*" [which is "the essence" of inspiration] *attended the entire process of the genesis of Scripture* [which is to be "sharply distinguished" from inspiration]!! And strange to say this confusion comes immediately after this solemn warning: "IT IS IMPORTANT that distinguishable ideas should be connoted by distinct terms, and that the terms themselves should be fixed in a definite sense!"—*Review*, p. 225.

criticism finds are by no means explicable as lapses of the pen. They are too closely bound with the warp and woof of the record. Structural variations,* dislocations of the narrative,† the transposition of events,‡ in some instances the duplication of the same event or saying in the same narrative,§ these surely

* As in the reports given respectively by Matthew and Luke of the Sermon on the Mount—Matt. v. 7; Luke vi. 20 f. Compare also the structure, introductions, contents, and forms of the discourses, &c., recorded in Matt. xii. 22 f; Mark iii. 20 f; Luke xi. 14 f; also in Matt. x. 1 f; Mark vi. 7 f; Luke ix. 1 f; also in Matt. xviii. 1—35; Mark ix. 33—50; Luke ix. 46—50.

† *E.g.* in Matt. (x. 1 f.) the ordination of the Twelve comes some time (cf. xi. 1 f.) *before* the events recorded in ch. xii. 1—21; whereas in Mark (ii. 23—iii. 12) and Luke (vi. 1 f.) they follow, though at no very long interval. Again, the contents of chs. viii.—ix. come considerably before (cf. ix. 35 f.; xi. 1 f., 20 f.) the events of ch. xii.; whereas in Mark and Luke the order is totally reversed, the events of Matt. xii. being recorded in Mark ii. 23 f.; iii. 1—35; Luke vi. 1—19 (*p. c.* Matt. xii. 22 f. not until Luke xi. 14 f.), and the events of Matt. viii. 18—ix. 26, in Mark iv. 35—v. 43, and Luke viii. 22 f. Again, the calling of Matthew, which in Mark (the same order substantially in Luke) comes before the contents of ii. 23—v. 21, in Matthew comes after the parallel parts of the record.

‡ Note, *e.g.*, in Matthew the position of the Galilean tour, comparing the context of Matt. iv. 23 f. with the context of Mark i. 35 f.; Luke iv. 42 f.; the place of the Sermon on the Mount in Matt. (v. 1 f.), as compared with its place in Luke vi. 20 f.; the order of the three temptations in Matt. iv. 1 f., as compared with Luke iv. 1 f.

§ Cf., *e.g.*, Matt. v. 29 f. with xviii. 8 f.; ix. 32 f. with xii. 22 f.; v. 24 with xxiii. 22.

are not transcriptional deviations from the original autograph.

Still further, on the *ipsissima verba* original autograph theory, textual criticism, as it restores to us the purer, more original, form of the text, should tend to eliminate these discrepancies, and to bring the various representations into closer harmony with each other. What is the fact? The very reverse. The more corrupt the text the smoother it is, the more in harmony with itself, the more do we find both of verbal and material assimilation in parallel passages. The older and purer the text, the rougher we find it, the more striking are its individualities, the more sharply accentuated are the differences, the less conformity do we find to a standard of infallible exactitude.

Let me give you one or two examples: In Mark i. 2 f. we have two Old Testament citations from two prophets, the first from Malachi, and the second from Isaiah. In the received text citations are introduced with the formula: "As it is written in the prophets." The true reading, however, is: "As it is written *in Isaiah the prophet.*" * Here the false reading gave us absolute inerrancy. The true reading gives us at least an inexactitude, which, whatever else may be said of it, is not unqualifiedly favourable to the affirmation that

* So, of course, the Revised Version.

the name "Isaiah" in the New Testament always meant one particular man, and nobody else.

Again : In Mark ii. 26, we read in the Authorised Version (following the received text) that David " went into the house of God in the days of Abiathar, the high priest." As a matter of fact, Abiathar was not the high priest at the time, but Abimelech. The explanation which a literalistic exegesis has commonly offered of the statement is, that Abiathar became high priest afterward, and that he is called so here by anticipation. And we may grant that, following the less authentic text, such an explanation, though not the most probable, was not impossible. But unfortunately textual criticism comes in, and proves that the passage should be read : " when Abiathar was high priest "* which puts the whole explanation out of court at once. Transcription had corrected the historical accuracy out of the text ; criticism, doing its duty honestly, has put it back.

Once more : In Matthew (xix. 17), where the ruler asked our Lord : " Good Master, what good thing shall I do that I may have eternal life ? " Christ answered, according to the received text : " Why callest thou Me good ? " Mark and Luke both give precisely, verbally, the same answer. So far the theory of verbal

* So the Revised Version.

inspiration is safe. But unfortunately here again textual criticism finds that Matthew's text should read : " Why askest thou Me concerning that which is good " ? *—a difference not only in the words but in the thought, and indeed in the point and pith of the answer. Thus we see that the tendency of a more exact knowledge of the text is to accentuate the individuality and variations of the records, so far as the nearest approach even to our original autographs enables us to judge.

And now is it supposed that we solve all the difficulties connected with the preliminary processes in the building of the record, by throwing the responsibility for inerrancy on the final revision? Shall we say that the inspiration of the Gospel of Luke, *e.g.*, is to be sought for—not in the material, not in the documents which he confessedly used ; but in the editorial compilation and elaboration of the material ? †   Surely this is a most unsatisfactory solution.   Of all the make-shifts, to which the theory of absolute inerrancy compels its adherents, this is to my mind the weakest. Inspiration a mere matter of editing and proofreading, of correction and revision, crossing out and touching up with the pen an uninspired record, and so making an inspired thing of it ! I challenge this conception here and now as unworthy, degrading, belittling, as more hostile

* So here, again, the Revised Version.   † See Note 2, p. 148.

to a robust, living faith than anything I know of short of rationalism! Inspiration—what is it? THEOPNEUSTIA! *The* BREATH *of God!* *The* LIFE *of God!* The pulsation of God's thought and heart all the way through. If you do not give me that, you give me stone for bread. "The words that I have spoken unto you are spirit and are life." The idea that inspiration resolves itself into the correction of a date, substituting one man's name for another, changing a number, inserting a caption—important as such particulars may be in their way—such an idea of inspiration is suitable only for Theology in Lilliputia.

But, as a matter of fact, where are we? What have we? Have we an infallible revision? Have we an inerrant result? Have we a New Testament, or an Old Testament, with absolutely no mistake, no inaccuracy, from beginning to end? I know of no respectable critic who claims that. Everybody will admit that, in the processes of transcription and transmission, at least, some error has crept into the book, some contradiction, some inaccuracy, which, as the matter stands, cannot be accepted as the exact statement of that particular matter. But is not that virtually to give up the whole position? What is inspiration for? Surely to advantage the reader.* But what

* "God gave His Word, not for the private use of the fifty or sixty chosen men to whom it was first revealed,

is the value of an infallible editorship which does not secure a permanently infallible text? Here is an error which has been in the text for fifteen centuries, and which, there cannot be much doubt, will stay there now for all the centuries to come. What difference does it make, so far as the readers of the past fifteen centuries and the readers of all future centuries are concerned, whether the error was in the original autograph or not? How does it affect the value of the record to-day, for you and for me, to say that the error which is there to-day was not there eighteen hundred years ago? Your inerrant autograph is an abstraction; your inerrant text is an abstraction. Does God hang His revelation on an abstraction? Does the present error destroy the inspiration of the Bible as we have it? We all say not. Then why should the original error destroy the inspiration of the Bible as it was first given? If absolute verbal infallibility were essential to inspiration, does not the loss of that infallibility imply the loss of that inspiration? If it were essential that the first copy should be inerrant in every possible particular; if without such inerrancy it could have no authority; why is not the same inerrancy essential to every copy, and where does the

but for the salvation of the innumerable company of the redeemed." Dr. E. P. Humphrey, *Second General Council of the Presbyterian Alliance*, 1880, p. 109.

authority of our present copies come from? *You* say : " A single error breaks down the Bible."* One comes up and points out an apparent error. Drs. Hodge and Warfield are constrained to admit that it has all the appearance of an error, † but that if we only had the original autograph, etc. He is a busy man, and cares very little for hypothetical abstractions, and replies : " On your own theory the Bible has all the appearance of being broken down by what has all the appearance of being an error. When you find your original autograph I shall be pleased to hear from you." You get the General Assembly to declare that, unless God gave an absolutely errorless Bible, He gave no Bible at all. Your people construe that to mean that, unless you have an absolutely errorless Bible, you have no Bible at all. What have you or they gained? I thank God that I am not shut up to any such conclusion ; and, most of all, I thank God that when an inquiring soul comes to me with his difficulties I do not have to shut him up to any such conclusion. There are spots on yonder sun ; do they stop its being a sun ? Why, science tells me that

---

* " A proved error in Scripture contradicts not only our doctrine, but the Scripture claims, and therefore its inspiration in making those claims." Drs. Hodge and Warfield, *The Presbyterian Review*, Vol. II., p. 245.

† See Note, p. 145.

they are a part of the solar economy, and that the sun is all the more a sun for the spots! How do I know that it may not be so with the Bible?

But the theory that all the errors in the text are surreptitious, that none of them are to be referred to the original autographs, is one which honest criticism finds itself unable to accept. Some, of course, might be accounted for in this way, but that the vast majority, and especially that those which present the most serious difficulties are later corruptions, is utterly out of the question. I have already shown that this theory fails us in the Gospels. Let us take one example out of the Epistles. In Galatians iii. 17, Paul says that the Law came 430 years after the Covenant with Abraham. But according to three express historical statements found elsewhere—to wit, God's prediction to Abraham (Gen. xv. 13), the statement of the Book of Exodus (xii. 40), and the statement of Stephen (Acts vii. 6)—the sojourning of the children of Israel in Egypt, and their bondage there, continued 400 or 430 (so Ex. *l. c.*) years, to which must be added the 200 years between the covenant with Abraham and Jacob's descent to Egypt, making more than 600 years from the Abrahamic covenant to the giving of the Law. According to the Hebrew Bible, and according to Stephen, Paul's chronology is at fault by about 200 years. And, unfortunately, we are precluded from falling back here on that convenient abstraction, the original autograph, by the unquestionable fact that, according to his customary rule, Paul is here following the Septuagint, which has added certain words to the Hebrew text in Exodus (*l. c.*) so as to make the 430 years include the sojourning in Canaan, along with the sojourning in Egypt. Now, as a question of criticism, Biblical and historical, I cannot help believing that the Hebrew text and Stephen are right here, and that the Septuagint and Paul are wrong. What am I to do? If I instruct my class that Paul's statement is infallibly inspired, I put Stephen in the wrong, I have the Old Testament passages to explain, and I have serious historical difficulties to remove.* Will you

---

* Of these difficulties, the most serious, and the only one to which I will now refer, lies in the extraordinary multiplication of the children of Israel in Egypt. The facts of the case, as given in Genesis and Exodus, are the following: 1. The number of the Israelites at the beginning of the sojourn in Egypt was seventy souls (Gen. xlvi. 27). —2. The number who went forth out of Egypt is given at "six hundred thousand on foot that were men, beside children" (Ex. xii. 37). This would give about three millions for the entire number.—3. This remarkable increase had taken place under the most grievous oppression and bondage (Ex. i. 7-14).—4. In the face also of concerted methods of extermination (Ex. i. 15-22). Many of the negative critics of the Bible, basing their deductions on the traditional chronology represented by the Septuagint, which

blame me if, instead of putting an artificial,
forced construction on such a passage in the
interests of an *à priori* theory, I prefer a
straightforward, manly, sober, reverent view
of the difficulty, like that which Prof. Beet has
taken in his Commentary?—"The above dis-

limits the sojourn of the Israelites in Egypt to 230 years,
have questioned the entire narrative. So, among others,
Bishop Colenso, who argued the case very skilfully and
forcibly from that point of view. Professor W. H. Green,
D.D., of Princeton, in his book, *The Pentateuch Vindicated
from the Aspersions of Bishop Colenso*, thus disposes of the
argument. Respecting the Septuagint reading of Ex. xii.
40, he says : "The gloss thus put upon this passage in
Exodus, as it seemed to have the authority of an inspired
Apostle in its favour in Gal. iii. 17, and as the genealogy of
Moses (Ex. vi. 16-20) appeared to preclude the supposition
that 430 years were spent in Egypt, became the well-nigh
universal view of the case. It still has its advocates,
though the leading Biblical scholars of Europe have abandoned
it." On the passage in Galatians, Dr. Green says: "This
language of the Apostle, however, does not appear to us to
be decisive of the point at issue. The interval of time is
only incidentally mentioned. *Precision of statement regarding
it was of no consequence to his argument.*" And on the chronology itself Dr. Green delivers this judgment: "The
evidence is, we think, *conclusive* that the *abode in Egypt
lasted* 430 *years*. This is the *natural sense* of Ex. xii. 40,
and *none would ever think of extracting a different meaning
from it*, but for reasons found outside of the verse itself.
. . . . The verse makes no allusion to Canaan, but only
to Egypt." In a subsequent chapter he shows how a term
of 430 years in Egypt meets all the requirements of the
narrative touching the multiplication of the nation, etc.
His whole argument is a striking illustration of the fact
that honest criticism yields in the end the best apologetic
results.—See pp. 117 f., 141 f., of *The Pentateuch Vindicated*.

cussion warns us not to try to settle questions of Old Testament historical criticism by casual allusions in the New Testament. All such attempts are unworthy of scientific Biblical scholarship. By inweaving His words to man in historic fact, God appealed to the ordinary laws of human credibility. These laws attest with absolute certainty the great facts of Christianity. And upon these great facts, and upon these only, rest both our faith in the Gospel and in God, and the authority of the Sacred Book. Consequently. . . . our faith does not require the absolute accuracy of every historical detail in the Bible, and is not disturbed by any error in detail which may be detected in its pages. At the same time, our study of the Bible reveals there an historical accuracy which will make us very slow to condemn as erroneous even unimportant statements of Holy Scripture. And in spite of any possible errors in small details or allusions, the Book itself remains to us as—in a unique and infinitely glorious sense—a literary embodiment of the Voice and Word of God." I most heartily say Amen to every line of that statement. It is the only tenable position to take.

This illustration brings up another point of importance in Biblical criticism. I refer to the use made of the Old Testament in the New. Without going into detail, let me call attention

11

to the fact that almost every possible way in which an Old Testament passage can be cited is adopted.*   As a rule, the citations follow the Septuagint, sometimes closely, sometimes loosely.   Sometimes the Seventy as cited is an exact translation of the original.   Sometimes it is a free, but faithful, rendering, giving the sense rather than the words.   Sometimes it is hardly a translation at all, but a paraphrase. Sometimes it gives a sense quite different from the original.   In making the citation, the New Testament writer sometimes quotes the Septuagint *verbatim.*   Sometimes he changes a word or two.   Sometimes the change brings the passage into closer conformity to the original Hebrew.   Sometimes the change introduces a variation both from the Hebrew, and from the Septuagint.   Sometimes the writer gives a new translation of the Hebrew, apparently his own.   I appeal to every candid student of these facts whether they comport with the notion of a rigorous verbal infallibility. To my mind they are quite conclusive of the contrary.   Calvin himself, referring to the deviation of the Seventy, as cited in Heb. xi. 21, from the Masoretic Hebrew text, says of the Apostolic use of the Old Testament: "The Apostle does not hesitate to accommodate to his own purpose (*non dubitat suo instituto*

* See D. M. Turpie, *The Old Testament in the New,* p. 266 f.

accommodare) what was commonly received. He wrote, indeed, to the Jews ; but to those who, being dispersed through various countries, had exchanged their national language for Greek. We know that in such a matter the Apostles were not very scrupulous (*non adeo fuisse scrupulosos*)," by which, of course, Calvin means that they were not careful about exactitude in all matters of detail. " In the thing itself," he adds, " there is but little difference." *

* It may be well to add here that, rigid in some respects as was Calvin's dogma of inspiration as set forth in his *Institutes*, though by no means as rigid as the later dogma, his attitude became very much freer when brought face to face with the particular problems of criticism. So rationalistic, indeed, did his treatment of the Old Testament seem to the more orthodox Lutherans of his day, that they charged him with Judaizing. One of them calls him *Calvinus Judaizans* (Aeg. Hunnius, *Vit.* 1593). Another accuses him of interpreting the passages about the Messiah and the Trinity in the sense of the Jews and the Socinians (see reff. in reuss, *History of the New Testament*, § 550). To the phrase, ἵνα πληρωθῇ in connection with O. T. citations, he gave so elastic an interpretation, that this, too, was denounced as rationalistic (*see* Tholuck on *Calvin as an Interpreter*, Bibl. Repos. ii., p. 541 ff.). He recognises an occasional inaccuracy in the text. On Matt. xxvii. 9, he says : " The passage itself plainly shows that the name of Jeremiah has been put down by mistake instead of Zechariah." He is, at least, not anxious to trace it back to the original autograph. " How the name of Jeremiah crept in, he says, I do not know, nor do I give myself much trouble to inquire (*nec anxie laboro*)." On Luke xxiv. 36, and elsewhere, he recognises contradictions, but uniformly

I have thus far sought to show that the theory of an *ipsissima verba* infallibility in Scripture fails when brought to the test of the best assured conclusions of criticism. It remains to take a brief look at the positive side of the question. For, allow me to say, that to us, even as to you—nay, to us even more than it can be to you—who say with Drs. Hodge and Warfield that "the essence of inspiration was superintendence," inspiration has a very positive side ; is a massive, all-controlling, overwhelmingly predominant fact, throughout the very warp and woof of the Bible from beginning to end. Inspiration is not to be measured by the trifles which have passed under our review. A trifle, to be sure, may be a fact; and if a fact, it is a sin to deny it, whether small as an atom or big as Jupiter. And if anywhere we are to bow before the facts it is in the sphere of Divine truth. It is not, as Professor Briggs

dismisses them as of no importance, leaving as they do the substance of the narrative unaffected. He doubts the Petrine authorship of the Second Epistle, and cannot be prevailed upon to acknowledge Paul as the author of the Epistle to the Hebrews (*ego ut Paulum agnoscam auctorem adduci nequeo*). "Only in his very earliest writings," says Reuss (*History of the New Testament*, § 335), "does he follow tradition." He was, in fact, a pioneer of the Higher Criticism, and it is only too evident that, if the question of confirming his election to one of our Biblical chairs were to come before us to-day, he would fail of getting a unanimous vote.

says, a pleasant task to point out errors in
Scripture. We do it only as the interests of
truth require, because we dare not handle the
word of God deceitfully. Nothing is worth
saving that cannot be saved honestly, not even
that Book. But we are at an infinite remove
from taking these as the measure of the Bible.
Cromwell showed his manliness in ordering the
painter to put in his portrait the wart on his
face; but who would dream of judging Cromwell by his wart? What are these trifling
inaccuracies in Scripture when compared with
the Burden of the Book? If one of the Gospel records varies from another in respect to
the *details* of a miracle, what difference does
it make if the miracle remains? If there are
minor incongruities in the narratives of
Christ's appearances after His resurrection,
is not the *fact* of his resurrection made all
the more certain even by these incongruities?
If Paul did—in very respectable company, too
—make a mistake of two hundred years in
stating his argument to the Galatians, what
has that to do with the argument? Does it
weaken in the slightest the sledge-hammer
blow with which he crushes Jewish legalism
dead for ever? If Stephen transposes certain
Old Testament incidents, or confuses certain
names, does that affect the convicting power of
his terrific arraignment of an apostate Israel?
Was not the power of the Holy Ghost in

every word that he spoke, even when least accurate?* Suppose that one of his hearers had undertaken to reply to him, saying: "You have said that Abraham left Haran after the death of his father, Terah; whereas, if you study the figures in Genesis, you will find that Terah must have lived fifty years or more in Haran after Abraham left. You were mistaken, also, in saying that Abraham bought the sepulchre of the sons of Hamor in Shechem. If you look into the matter a little more closely you will find that that was Jacob, and that Abraham bought his purchase at Hebron of

---

*It is one of the pitiful subterfuges of the mechanical theory that Stephen was not, or may not have been, inspired. Luke, forsooth, in his account of the external circumstances attending the discourse, was inspired, but Stephen not! And this in face of all that the inspired Luke says about Stephen, that he was "full of grace and power" (Acts vi. 8); that his opponents "were not able to withstand the wisdom and the Spirit by which he spake" (vi. 10); that during this same address, "all that sat in the council, fastening their eyes on him, saw his face as it had been the face of an angel" (vi. 15); that his unbelieving hearers "were cut to the heart, and they gnashed on him with their teeth" (vii. 54); that at the close, Stephen himself, "being full of the Holy Spirit, looked up steadfastly into heaven and saw the glory of God, and Jesus standing on the right hand of God" (vii. 55 f.). This man's inspiration, an open question at the least, to be denied if the exigencies of an infinitesimal literalistic inspiration requires it; but the words of the annalist, who thus introduces the discourse: "And the high priest said, Are these things so? And he said," potent with the essence itself of inspiration—supervision! Is not such a theory self-condemned?

Ephron the Hittite." But would that have silenced Stephen? Such a criticism on such a speech would have been like flinging a feather in the teeth of a cyclone.

God has not been afraid to commit the excellency of His treasure to earthen vessels. He is not alarmed lest the weakness of the vessel should be a damage to the treasure. He has not shrunk from risking His truth on the liabilities of traditions, translations, transcriptions, and their inevitable accompaniments of fallibility. He has not been concerned lest the popular misconceptions of a pre-Copernican astronomy, or of a pre-Lyellian geology, or of a pre-Linnæan botany, should compromise His revelation of Himself. I thank God that it is so. I rejoice that, Divine as is the Book, Divine as no other book is, it is still so thoroughly human; so beautifully threaded with the fibre of human nerve, thought, and sensibility; so sweetly veined with the crimson channels of the heart's blood, life, and experience. I rejoice that, supernatural as it is, supernatural as no other book is, it is still so thoroughly natural, that its literary life and growth blend so lovingly and harmoniously with the currents and processes of the world's divinely-appointed life and growth. I rejoice that God, when He speaks in the language of earth and by the mouth of His servants, comes so low down that He is not ashamed to use bad grammar, is not afraid of a barbarism or a solecism, does not shrink from an archaism or an anachronism, does not disdain an antediluvian setting for the doctrine of the Creation or the Fall, or what a scientist might derisively call a *Kindergarten* formula for the truth of Providence, or the Judgment. He does not hang eternal issues on details that are relatively insignificant. He has not so poised the Rock of Ages that the Higher or Lower Criticism, with pickaxe or crowbar, digging out a chronological inaccuracy here, or prizing off a historical contradiction there, is going to upset it. The critic may be all right, the crowbar may be all right, but the Rock of Ages is all right too, and it will stand fast for ever. Do not, I beseech you, charge upon God the priggish precision which makes as much of a molehill as of a mountain. God does not care to be honoured in that way. Do not degrade Him by requiring that He should poise before His earthly children as an intolerant, if not intolerable, Pedant, who insists on his *p's* and *q's* with no less vigour and pertinacity than on His godlike SHEMA : " Hear, O Israel ! " — or on His everlasting AMEN : " Verily, verily, I say unto you ! "

But what of the positive bearing of the conclusions of criticism on our conception of inspiration ? Take, *e.g.*, its conclusions in respect to the structure and contents of the

Synoptic Gospels. What do they teach us as to the fact of inspiration? They teach us that it is a much larger fact than the scholastic notion which resolves it into mere supervision. Its scope is much wider. It is the note of a supernatural age; an age in which supernatural forces were at work on an extensive scale; in which supernatural facts had been witnessed by multitudes, and had stamped their impressions on thousands of living souls; an age when supernatural charismata abounded in the Church; an age of miracles, of supernatural healings, of supernatural tongues. It was pre-eminently an age of prophetic inspiration, in which the Old Testament predictions were fulfilled: "And it shall be in the last days, saith God, I will pour forth of My Spirit *upon all flesh;* And your sons and your daughters shall prophesy, And your young men shall see visions, And your old men shall dream dreams; Yea, and on My servants, and on My handmaidens in those days will I pour forth of My Spirit; And they shall prophesy." * It was an age in which there was an order of prophets in the Church and a gift of prophesying in the churches. It was an age when Luke could say that "*many* have taken in hand to draw up a narrative concerning these matters which have been fulfilled [or fully established] among us "; an age which furnished Luke with that inimitable

* Acts ii. 14 f.

story of the Infancy, written nobody knows by
whom, perhaps, as Alford suggests, by Mary,
the mother of our Lord, but as plenarily
inspired, before Luke ever got hold of it, as
anything that Peter or John ever wrote ; an
age which furnished the fragment at the end
of Mark, written nobody knows by whom, but
attesting itself to the consciousness of the
Church to-day, as throughout the centuries, as
the inspired Word of God, as truly and as
fully such as all of Mark ; * an age which
furnished the pericope of the woman taken in
adultery, written nobody knows by whom, but
as full of Jesus as the diamond is full of the
sun ; † an age of inspired Christian hymns,
some of which have found their way into the
record, sung nobody knows by whom, but
sweet and grand as the apocalyptic melodies
of heaven's own Alleluias ; ‡ an age when, as
the appendix to John's Gospel declares, if all
the facts known respecting Christ were written,
the world itself would not contain the books
that should be written ; an age when we know
not how many inspired records and epistles

* See Revised Version at Mark xvi. 9 f.
† See Revised Version at John vii. 53—viii. 11.
‡ See 1 Cor. xiv. 26; Col. iii. 16; Eph. v. 19.   See exx.
in the songs of Mary, Zacharias, and Simeon (Lk. i. 46 f.,
67 f.; ii. 29 f. in Revised Version and Westcott and Hort;
also Eph. v. 14; 1 Tim. iii. 16, in Westcott and Hort.
Cf. Acts iv. 24 f.).   See Winer's *Grammar of the New Testament Diction*, § 68, 3, 4.

were written and lost ; * an age which built up
mighty Christian traditions, not like the dead,
dry petrifactions of Judaism, but fresh, living,
burning traditions, to which the Apostles
could appeal as instinct with vital energy and
authority.† Think you that in such an age
there would be any lack of inspiration for
building up the Gospel record? Look at the
quantity and the quality of the inspiration
which this view gives you; not the pedantic,
pedagogical supervision of " jots and tittles,"
but the grand, living expression of " the powers
of the world to come ;" not an occasional
spurt or spasm, but a great dynamic, œcumenical fact; not the flow of a few artesian
wells, but a mighty tide, surging out of the
great supernatural deep. What a broad,
impregnable base you have here for the
Gospel record! What a great cloud of
witnesses ! What palpable energy and vital-
ity of conviction palpitating through every
line of the manifold testimony? What
overwhelming, convincing power in the con-
sentaneous strength of the Gospel witness to
its own transcendent facts, when this witness
is found to rest on no artificial support, is

* See 1 Cor. v. 9 ; 2 Cor. x. 10, xi. 28; 2 Thess. ii. 15,
iii. 17; Phil. iii. 18 (Col. iv. 16? more probably the
extant Ep. to the Ephesians) ; 3 John iii. 9.—See Salmon's
Introduction to the New Testament, Lecture XX.

† See Luke i. 2 ; 1 Cor. xi. 2, 23 ; 2 Thess. ii. 15 ; iii. 6 ;
2 Tim. i. 13; 2 Peter ii. 21, iii. 2; Jude 3, 17.

secured by no mechanical uniformity, but
comes to us through what Professor Beet
calls "the ordinary laws of human credibility,"
bearing those marks of honesty, independence,
frankness, individuality, spontaneity, internal
verisimilitude, which everywhere and always
guarantee the truth of human testimony! Is it
not the claim and glory of the Gospel story
that it combines the dignity and authority of a
heavenly recital with the piquant frankness,
the homelike *naïveté* of the conversational
fireside tale ; here and there, it may be, con-
tradicting itself in small matters, breaking out
into artless variations and impulsive inconsistencies, but all the more surely thereby
winning its way to the faith and love of the
heart ?

The most important question of all still
remains to be considered. What is inspiration—not in itself, but as a fact, as a
characteristic of the Bible? In giving my
answer to this question, I know no better
course to take than to follow the line of
thought in the first chapter of our Confession of Faith, perhaps the noblest chapter
in that immortal document. Let me ask your
attention to what is most essential in that
magnificent statement of the truth respecting
Scripture. "Although the light of nature,
and the works of creation and Providence, do
so far manifest the goodness, wisdom, and

power of God, as to leave men inexcusable ; yet they are not sufficient to give that knowledge of God, and of His will, which is necessary unto salvation." Let us ponder that statement a moment. Why was Scripture given ? The answer of our Confession is : Because "the light of nature was not sufficient." Sufficient for what ? "To give [a certain] knowledge." Knowledge of what ? Of botany ? chemistry ? geography ? By no means. The light of nature *is* sufficient for that. It is not sufficient, however, "*for the knowledge* OF GOD "—that Great Infinite Being with whom, as spiritual immortal beings, we have to do ; "*and of* HIS WILL "—that expression of God's eternal thoughts and purpose which most essentially concerns our spiritual welfare and our eternal destiny ; and still more explicitly, "not sufficient for *that* knowledge of God which is necessary "—for what ? For science ? for art ? for civilisation ? necessary to fill a cyclopædia ? to equip a college graduate ?—nay, "but which is *necessary* UNTO SALVATION." What is all secular knowledge compared with "that knowledge of God which is necessary unto salvation "? That was the great need of the world ; it was to supply that need that when the light of nature failed man, God interposed. *Therefore* it pleased the Lord, at sundry times,*

* Revised Version, "by divers portions."

and in divers manners, TO REVEAL HIM-
SELF." Mark that! Not in the first instance to give a book, not to transmit a
revelation *about* Himself, not to write or
cause to be written, a series of definitions,
logical categories, abstract propositions relating
to His person, His nature, His attributes; but
"*to reveal* HIMSELF"—actually, factually, in
living deed, as well as by the living Word; by
theophanies, by covenants, by dispensations;
by orders, institutions, structures—legislative,
administrative, civil, religious; by sacrifices
and sacraments, Urim and Thummim, blood
and Shekinah; by mediations of grace and
life most various, touching, and sublime—
didactic, devotional, priestly, prophetic; by
dream, vision, psalm, symbol, type, miracle—
a golden chain of Divine manifestations and
interpositions reaching down through the
centuries; every new link charged with more
of God—God in it all—God Himself—God in
person; the Power of God, the Heart of God,
the Life of God in everything; and ALL FOR
SALVATION! Emphasize that again! *Revelation*
and *Redemption* — twin divinities, advancing
together, side by side, step by step, every step
ablaze with Deity! the Divine processes widen-
ing with the suns, more, and more, and ever
more of God in everything until at last the
climax is reached—the Word becomes flesh;
the Son of God is born on earth, lives—suffers

—dies—rises again—ascends to the right hand of the Majesty on high, to reign King of kings, and Lord of lords, God blessed for ever. Amen!

Here in these great facts, these great historic processes, these theophanies of glory, these miracles of power and love, these supernatural interventions of redeeming grace, we have God revealing Himself. That precisely, as our Confession puts it, is the primal fact. Here you have the material of the Word of God, the stuff of inspiration, the substance of the Gospel. Paul's definition of the Gospel is just that : " The Power of God unto Salvation." Not a thing of power, not a mighty system, not a tremendous engine, but *Dunamis,* Power, God's Power, Personal Omnipotence, at work as Omnipotence, saving the world. " My Father *worketh* hitherto, and I *work.*" That is Redemption. That is Revelation for Redemption. The life of the Revelation is there, the power of the Revelation is there, in that Divine working ; not in words, not in definitions, not in abstract statements— how much of God can you put into words ? How much of the Eternal can you pack into a definition ? How much of the Infinite can you squeeze into a dogma ?—No, not in these, but in those stupendous supernatural forth-puttings of God Himself, which blazon their way all along from Eden to Golgotha.

So much for the first step—the redemptive revelation of Himself by God. "It pleased the Lord," first of all, thus "to reveal Himself, and to declare His will unto His Church." What next? "And *afterward*," mark the order, the dependence, and the purpose, "and afterward for the better preserving and propagating of the truth, and for the more sure establishment and comfort of the Church against the corruption of the flesh, and the malice of Satan, and of the world, to commit the same wholly unto writing, which maketh the Holy Scripture to be most necessary; those former ways of God's revealing His will unto His people being now ceased." The Bible is thus the written record of the revelation. What, then, is the object of the record? Generically and primarily the object of the record is the same with the object of the Revelation, to wit : Salvation. Specifically the record is given for three purposes subordinate to the great generic purpose : (1) To interpret the Revelation, or, in the language of the Confession, "to declare God's will" in the Revelation. For man, alas! is ignorant, blinded, besotted by sin, and needs to have this wondrous Divine Drama of Redemption explained. (2) To perpetuate the Revelation, "those former ways of God's revealing His will having now ceased." (3) To apply the Revelation ; or to make it effectual against the trinity of evil—the world, the flesh, and Satan.

What now is the function of Inspiration? In a word, it is to mediate the Revelation; to interpret, to record, to apply it; to put us, to put all generations, under the immediate power of those Divine realities; so far as possible to bring us face to face with this incomparable drama of Power and Love Divine, *face to face with God revealing Himself.* All through the ages the Spirit of God was teaching one and another to understand, to interpret, to record, to apply that wondrous process. There, then, you have the Revelation; here the Inspiration. There the supernatural history; here the supernatural record. There the fact; here the story. There Sinai; here Exodus. There Bethlehem, Galilee, Calvary, Olivet; here Matthew, Mark, Luke, John. There Pentecost; here the Acts. And as the Revelation was building, so the Book was building. As that became high and broad, this became rich and full. And so the Book became the double of the deed. By the Divine correlation of energy, the life and power of the one became the life and power of the other. The Facts burn in the Words. The living History throbs in the living Record. And so to-day, and throughout all time, in all that makes the Bible the power of God unto salvation, it is the Voice of God, the Word

12

of God, the supreme, the only, the infallible, authority.*

That is what the Bible teaches concerning itself. It is part of the supernatural, Divine process of saving a lost world, of rehabilitating a ruined humanity. Inspiration is the formal factor in that process, as Revelation is the material factor. Thus regarded, I have no hesitation in saying that the Bible is inspired wholly, inspired through and through. The men are inspired, as Professor Stowe said. The thoughts are inspired, as Professor Briggs says. The words are inspired, as Professor Hodge has said. These are " the sacred writings which are able to *make wise* UNTO SALVATION, *through faith which is in Jesus Christ.*" "Every Scripture is inspired of God, and profitable for teaching, for reproof, for correction, for discipline which is in righteousness ; that the man of God may be complete, furnished completely unto every good work."

---

* I take pleasure in referring to the admirable statement of this historic and literary relation of Revelation and Inspiration in Drs. Hodge and Warfield's article on Inspiration, in *The Presbyterian Review*, Vol. II. For more complete and systematic discussion of the subject, see Dr. G. P. Fisher's *Nature and Object of Revelation* (Scribner : New York) ; Dr. A. B. Bruce : *The Chief End of Revelation* (Hodder & Stoughton) ; Dr. G. T. Ladd : " *The Doctrine of Sacred Scripture,* and *What is the Bible ?* (C. Scribner's Sons, New York) ; Dr. W. Sanday : *The Oracles of God* (Longmans, Green, & Co.).

That is what Inspiration is for, for training
and completing in the Divine life. How can
error in chronology, or physical science, affect
that process ? " The words that I have
spoken unto you are spirit, and are life."
Yes ! in these inspired words there is a
Divine pneumatic power such as no other
words have. They are Spirit-words, Life-
words. " Which things we teach, not in
words that man's wisdom teacheth, but which
the Spirit teacheth." What things ? Read
the context. " Whatever things God prepared for them that love Him." " The deep
things of God." " The things that were freely
[graciously] given to us of God." These are
the things about which Inspiration concerns
itself. God's things, God's deepest things,
God's best things, the things which have the
most, the deepest, of God in them." " *These*
things," says the Apostle of God in them,
" we teach *in words* which the Spirit of God
teacheth." Most assuredly ! Who can doubt
it ? I believe in that declaration of Paul's
with all my heart. I could not help believing
it if Paul had never said it. As I read what
the Bible says about God, about Christ, about
the Spirit, about man, sin, salvation, about
holiness, duty, life, death, eternity, I feel, to
the depths of my being, that the very words
thrill with Divinity ; they glow with the
ardours of the heaven above me ; they are

instinct with the power of an endless life ; the majesty of eternity is in their rhythm ; deep calleth unto deep in the thunders of their diapason ; the pathos of the blessed Comforter is in their stillest, smallest voice ; the very balm of Paradise is shed upon them ; even upon their anomalies rests the glory of the Shekinah ; as they pass before my eye they are radiant with the One altogether lovely ; as they echo in my heart-strings they are vocal with God.

It is most strange to me that our theologies have not before now found the secret of Inspiration in that transcendent passage of Paul, from which I have just cited a few lines—the clearest, the fullest, the profoundest treatment of the subject that has ever been given. Let me give the whole passage (1 Cor. ii. 6—16) : "Howbeit we speak wisdom among them that are fully grown : yet a wisdom not of this world, nor of the rulers of this world, who are coming to nought : but we speak God's wisdom in a mystery, even the wisdom that hath been hidden, which God fore-ordained before the worlds unto our glory : which none of the rulers of this world hath known ; for had they known it, they would not have crucified the Lord of glory : but as it is written : things which eye saw not, and ear heard not, and which entered not into the heart of man, whatsoever things God prepared for them that love Him. But unto us God revealed them

through the Spirit: for the Spirit searcheth
all things, yea, the deep things of God. For
who among men knoweth the things of a man,
save the spirit of the man, which is in him?
even so the things of God none knoweth, save
the Spirit of God. But we received not the
spirit of the world, but the Spirit which is
from God; that we might know the things
that were freely given to us of God. Which
things also we speak, not in words which man's
wisdom teacheth, but which the Spirit teacheth; combining spiritual things with spiritual
words [or, marg.—interpreting spiritual things
to spiritual men]. Now the natural [or: un-
spiritual, Gr. psychical] man receiveth not
the things of the Spirit of God: for they are
foolishness unto him; and he cannot know
them, because they are spiritually judged [or,
examined]. But he that is spiritual judgeth
[or, examineth] all things, and he himself is
judged [or, examined] of no man. For who
hath known the mind of the Lord, that he
should instruct Him? But we have the mind
of Christ."

That is Inspiration. How, then, shall
we characterise it? " Verbal" Inspiration?
" Supervisional?" " Official?" " Plenary?"
"Dynamic?" Why not take Paul's word at once,
which sums up what is most real in all these
designations? " PNEUMATIC INSPIRATION!"
There you have it all. There you have not

only Paul's word, but Christ's. "The words that I have spoken unto you are *Pneuma*." Make that your watchword, and you can hold the fort against all comers.

Pneumatic Inspiration : what does it mean ?

1. THE SPIRIT OF GOD is the primary, the vital, the essential, factor.

2. *The spirit of man* is the co-efficient : that in man which is the organ of God, and of all Divine Reality.

3. The contents of Inspiration are *pneumatic realities.* And what does the Apostle say of these ? (i.) They have their foundations in the depths of the Godhead. They are "the deep things of God." (ii.) They are above and beyond all secular science. "Not of this world" [or, age : *αἰών, saeculum*]. (iii.) They are the embodiment of a Divine Philosophy. "We speak God's Wisdom." (iv.) They are attained through a Divine initiation. "In a mystery." (v.) They date from the past eternity. "Fore-ordained before the worlds." (vi.) They fill the future eternity. "Prepared for them that love Him." (vii.) They are supra-sensual. "Eye saw not, ear heard not." (viii.) They are supra-psychical. "The natural [psychical] man receiveth them not." (ix.) They are supra-rational. "Which entered not into the heart of man." (x.) They are the peculiar province of the Spirit, "who explores the depths of God." "None knoweth them save

the Spirit of God." (xi.) They are freighted with Divine Grace. "Freely given to us of God." (xii.) They culminate in spiritual perfection. "Unto our glory."

4. The processes by which they are apprehended are pneumatic. "They are spiritually judged."

5. The utterances, by which they are expressed, are pneumatic, theopneustic. "In words which the Spirit teacheth." "Combining spiritualities with spiritualities."

6. And to crown all this all-pervading, all-assimilating Pneuma is the Mind of the Lord. "We have the mind of Christ."

Pneumatic Inspiration! Is it not just that? Do you ask for characteristics of Inspiration? There they are. Tests of Inspiration? What more could you wish for? Safeguards of inspiration? Are these not enough? If these will not guarantee the inspiration of the Bible, what will? According to our Confession, the inspiration of Scripture is a self-witnessing fact. "We may be moved and induced by the testimony of the Church to a high and reverend esteem for the holy Scripture; and the heavenliness of the matter, the efficacy of the doctrine, the majesty of the style, the consent of all the parts, the scope of the whole (which is to give all glory to God), the full discovery it makes of the only way of man's salvation, the many other incomparable excellencies, and the entire perfection thereof, are arguments whereby it doth abundantly evidence itself to be the Word of God ; yet, notwithstanding, our full persuasion and assurance of the infallible truth, and Divine authority thereof, is from the inward work of the Holy Spirit, bearing witness, by and with the Word, in our hearts." " The Supreme Judge, . . . in whose sentence we are to rest, can be no other but the Holy Spirit, speaking in the Scriptures." * Does not that which is of the Spirit evidence itself ? With this pneumatic conception of the Book, can we be in doubt about the inspiration, about the quality, contents, scope, purpose of the inspiration ? Can we have any trouble about verifying it ? The Bible is a pneumatic Book. The groundwork, the substance, all that makes the Book what it is, is pneumatic.† The warp and woof of it is *pneuma*. Its fringes run off, as was inevitable, into the secular, the material, the psychic. Can we not, as persons of common intelligence even, much more with the internal witness of the Spirit to aid us, discriminate between the fringe and the warp and woof ? Do not the

* *The Confession of Faith*, Chap. I., Secs. V., X. Compare the Larger Catechism, Qu. 2, 3, 4, and Answers.

† See The Larger Catechism, Qu. 5 (The Shorter Catechism, Qu. 3) and Answer. " *Qu.* What do the Scriptures principally teach ? *Ans.* The Scriptures principally teach what man is to believe concerning God, and what duty God requires of man."

" spiritualities " and the " heavenlinesses "
of Scripture distinguish themselves from all
that is lower, as the steady shining of the
everlasting stars from the fitful gleaming of
earth's fire-flies ? Even if the task of discriminating were immeasurably harder than it is,
we should not complain. God lays on us in
many matters, in matters, too, of great practical moment, the responsibility of separating
the things that differ. " Why, even of your-
selves judge ye not what is right ? " This
responsibility is a part of life's discipline. It
is not God's way to do all our thinking for us.
His training is not a process of cram.

Let me ask your attention to these weighty
words of Mr. Gladstone : " No doubt there
will be those who will resent any association
between the idea of a Divine Revelation and
the possibility of even the smallest intrusion of
error in the vehicle. But ought they not to
bear in mind that we are bound by the rule of
reason to look for the same methods of procedure in this great matter of a special provision
of Divine knowledge for our needs as in the
other parts of the manifold dispensation under
which Providence has placed us ? Now, that
method or principle is one of sufficiency, not
. perfection ; of sufficiency for the attainment of
practical ends, not of conformity to ideal
standards. Bishop Butler, I think, would wisely
tell us that we are not the judges, and that we

are quite unfit to be the judges, what may be the proper amount, and the just condition of any of the aids to be afforded us in passing through the discipline of life. I will only remark that this default of ideal perfection, this use of a twilight instead of a noonday blaze, may be adapted to our weakness, and may be among the appointed means of exercising our faith. But what belongs to the present occasion is to point out that if probability and not demonstration marks the Divine guidance of our paths in life as a whole, we are not entitled to require that when the Almighty in His mercy makes a special addition by revelation to what He has already given to us of knowledge in Nature and in Providence, that special gift should be unlike His other gifts, and should have all its lines and limits drawn out with mathematical precision."*

That is the only rational, the only philosophic, the only Scriptural ground to take. It is the ground of our Confession. The inspiration of the Bible is pneumatic, not psychic, not secular. The infallibility of the Bible is pneumatic, not psychic, not secular. It is the infallibility of practical sufficiency, not the infallibility of absolute ideality. It is an " infallible rule," standard measure. What

* *The Impregnable Rock of Holy Scripture.* By W. E. Gladstone.

does that mean ? I have a yard-stick, a three-foot rule. As such it is perfect, all-sufficient. If I make a mistake in measuring yards or feet with it, it will be altogether my own fault. And yet, perhaps, it is notched, it is cracked, some of the inch lines are blurred ; one or two may possibly be slightly inexact. If I were to apply the microscope to it, I should no doubt find flaws in it. If I were to try it for microscopic measurements, it would fail me. But as a yard-stick, as a three-foot measure, it is infallible. So with the Bible. Its infallibility is not a microscopic infinitesimal infallibility respecting all particular things in the heavens above or in the earth beneath, or in the waters under the earth. It is an infallible *rule of faith ;* *i.e.,* of Christian faith, of Gospel faith, of the faith which is necessary to salvation.

That, as I have shown, is the teaching of Scripture itself. That is plainly the teaching of our Confession. It is so interpreted by the most competent authorities. Dr. Laidlaw, Professor of Theology in the New College in Edinburgh, in a recent address on " The Westminster Confession in the Light of the Present Desire for Revision," speaking of the Chapter on the Scriptures, says that " it refrains from detailed specification as to the authorship, age, or literary character of the canonical books. Not making these matters essential to faith, it thus leaves open what has been called, perhaps rather broadly, the whole field of Biblical Criticism. It deals in the same manner with all details as to mode and degree of inspiration, which could be consistently left open by those who accept the Scriptures as the infallible rule of faith and duty. Once more, while claiming for the original Scriptures such immediate inspiration and such providential care as fits them for their purpose, it has refrained from such assertion of verbal inerrancy as Biblical scholarship disallows."*

The leaders of English and Scotch Presbyterianism are well-nigh a unit on this point. Dr. Blaikie, the President of the Presbyterian Alliance, and of whom I need say no more, was solicited last year to sign a paper condemning the views of Dr. Bruce and Dr. Dods. He declined to do so on the ground that while strongly maintaining the fact of Inspiration, he could not accept the rigid view which takes inspiration to mean inerrancy. " Well-known facts in the actual structure and contents of Scripture seem to me to forbid it."† Dr. Rainy is well known as Principal of the Free College of Edinburgh and the leader of the Free Church. Last year, in a speech in the Free Assembly, he

* *British Weekly*, November 13, 1890, p. 34.
† *British Weekly*, October 30, 1890, p. 3.

thus defined his personal position. I quote from an abstract in *The British Weekly* of June 6, 1890: "He started with the inerrancy of Scriptures, even in details, as that which he was inclined to hold. Only he refused to impose it on others; out and out he refused to do so, especially upon his students. He did so partly because he thought such matters despicable, but also because Scripture itself did not seem to have it much at heart to make them sure of accuracy of this kind; rather, it seemed conspicuously to refuse to do so, and any quotations to the contrary were mistakes." In the English Presbyterian Church, during the recent discussions of the New Confession of Faith, Principal Dykes, of the Presbyterian College in London, the leading theologian of the Church, Dr. Monro Gibson, who is accepted as the incoming Moderator, and other leaders, pronounced decisively against the theory of inerrancy. Two years ago, when Dr. Dods was nominated for the Exegetical Chair of New College, Edinburgh, declarations like the following were quoted against him: "I believe the Scriptures contain an infallible rule of faith and life. I believe they are the authoritative records of the revelations which God has made, but it is impossible to affirm that all the statements contained in Scripture are strictly accurate; impossible, that is, to

claim for Scripture an absolute infallibility."
He was elected by an overwhelming majority.
That is enough to show where the Free Church
stands on this particular issue.

Brethren, our Church can not afford to go
beyond Scripture, beyond our own Confession,
or beyond our sister churches, on this question.
We hear about " dangerous errors," views and
utterances which tend to unsettle faith. Let
me tell you where the danger lies, as it confronts me in my work from year to year. It
lies in putting the Bible in a false position, in
claiming for it what it does not claim for itself.
It lies in *a priori* assumptions respecting inspiration and infallibility, which are not borne
out by the facts. It lies in holding up
your iron-clad dogma of verbal inspiration and
literalistic infallibility against the advances
made by an humble, prayerful, reverent investigation and criticism of Scripture as the Word
of God. I have nothing to say in behalf of a
bald, agnostic, materialistic naturalism, or of
an arbitrary, capricious rationalism, which,
with *a priori* dogmatism, denies the supernatural, belittles or expunges sin and salvation,
eliminates out of history God's revelation of
Himself, evaporates out of the Bible its pneumatic inspiration, chops up its contents into
lifeless fragments, and sweeps away book after
book into the abyss of legend and myth. When
the Biblical Criticism of our theological semi-

naries is found to be engaged in that business, when it comes in conflict with the Bible's own claims to pneumatic inspiration, then it will be time to sound the alarm, then it will be time for action. But, on the other hand, a dogma of inspiration, and of the authority of Scripture, which, in its mistaken zeal, refuses to recognise accomplished results, antagonises the most enlightened, devout, and believing Biblical scholarship of the day, puts the ban on all inquiry which will not bow to its rigid literalism and mechanicalism, such a dogma is in our day, whatever it may have been in the past, an obstruction to faith, a menace to the unity and peace of the Church, an arrest of the healthy growth of Christian science, and a serious blight on the free, robust, symmetrical development of the Christian life. You protest against the unsettling of faith. You do well. But they also do well who protest against keeping up needless barriers to faith. You condemn criticism which destroys belief in the Scriptures as the Word of God. But beware of including in your condemnation the criticism which helps to make such belief in the Scriptures possible. You may be sure that as long as you tie up faith in the Bible with faith in a secular inspiration, as long as you hang the infallible authority of Scripture as the rule of faith on the infallible accuracy of every particular word and clause in the

Book, as long as you exalt the Bible to the same pinnacle of authority in matters respecting which God has given us clearer, fuller, more exact revelations elsewhere, as in matters respecting which the Bible is the only revelation, the irrepressible conflict between faith and science will go on, and the Drapers and Whites of each generation will have their new chapters to add to the record. Every new discovery in science or in archæology that seems to contradict some particular statement will produce a panic. Every advance in criticism will tend to unsettle the faith of somebody whom your teaching has led to confound the form with the substance. Having learned from you that the shell is part of the kernel, and finding that he cannot keep the shell, he will end by throwing away both shell and kernel.

For one I mean to do my part in putting an end to this mistaken defence of Divine Revelation. Shipwrecks of faith without number have been caused by it. It is the very thing, according to his own confession, that made an unbeliever of the most brilliant scholar of France, perhaps of the world to-day, Ernest Rénan. It is the very thing that drove into infidelity the strongest champion of the popular infidelity of England, who died the other day in his unbelief, Charles Bradlaugh. So testifies his own brother, a believer. But for this the iridescent declamation of Robert Ingersoll in our own country, with his "Mistakes of Moses," would collapse like a pricked balloon. The Christianity of our day cannot afford to fight the battle of the Book along that line. The Presbyterianism of our country cannot afford to put itself in antagonism to the most enlightened as well as devout Christian scholarship of the day. It cannot afford to put the yoke of bondage to an exploded relic of post-Reformation scholasticism on the consciences of our young men, alive as they are to the gains of reverent and careful study of the Book, and sensitive as they cannot fail to be to the humiliation of such bondage. It can not afford to silence the larger, profounder, more Scriptural restatements of revealed truth made imperative by improved methods of Biblical research. Nor can it afford to precipitate any issue on our churches, the surest result of which will be to foment suspicion, to drive out the spirit of charity and of justice, to gender misunderstanding and alienation between our chairs of instruction and our pulpits and pews, and to widen the gap between honest inquiry and earnest faith.

13

BIBLICAL SCHOLARSHIP
AND INSPIRATION.

II.

By HENRY PRESERVED SMITH, D.D.,

*Professor of Hebrew in Lane Theological Seminary,
Cincinnati.*

BIBLICAL SCHOLARSHIP AND INSPIRATION.

THE natural theory concerning an inspired book is illustrated by the Mohammedans. The Prophet of Mecca, in his observation of Jews and Christians (in whom he recognised worshippers of the true God), discovered their Scriptures to be the source of their religion. He classified them therefore as "book-people," and endeavoured to construct a similar sacred code for his own followers. The result is the Koran, whose contrast with the Bible is in many respects remarkable. Throughout this book God appears as the speaker. Its contents are made known to the prophet by direct revelation, and it is never tired of emphasizing its own infallibility. Yet the discrepancies are so marked that they did not escape the notice of the author himself, and he propounded the theory, afterwards elaborated by the commentators, that a later revelation must abrogate an earlier one. He confessed forgetfulness also,*

* "Whatever verses We cancel or cause thee to forget, We give thee better in their stead, or the like thereof." —Koran II. 100, quoted by Sir William Muir, *The Corân*, p. 41.

and in one instance avowed that Satan had insinuated a false revelation into his mind.*

¶ The transmission of this book is well known. No particular care was taken of the revelations during the author's life, or for some time after his death. As the number of his "companions" was diminished by death, the danger of losing the revelations became evident, and with the lapse of time discrepancies in the various readings became marked. War threatened to break out between parties who swore allegiance to different readings.† One of Mohammed's amanuenses was therefore commissioned to collect the fragments "from date-leaves and tablets of white stone, and from the breasts of men," to which other traditions add from fragments of parchment or paper, pieces of leather, and the shoulder or rib-bones of camels or goats. As this standard text was corrupted by careless copyists, probably under the influence of still living tradition, the Caliph Othman had an authorised edition made by a committee of scholars. " Transcripts [of this] were multiplied and forwarded to the chief cities in the empire, and the previously-existing copies were all, by the Caliph's com-

---

* The "two Satanic verses," cf. Muir, *Life of Mahomet* (1877), p. 86 sqq.

† Or different wordings, for the transmission was still largely oral.

mand, committed to the flames." * The text was still unvocalised, the points not being added until about fifty years later.

Now the point I wish to make is this: We have full knowledge of these details concerning the Koran; we know its discrepancies, its careless editing, the violent means taken to secure uniformity in its text, the late origin of its vowel points; the Arab scholars know these also, for it is from them that we get the information. Yet the Arab theory maintains the following points:

1. The Koran is eternal in its original essence and a necessary attribute of God.

2. It was written down in heaven on a "treasured tablet," from which it was communicated piecemeal to Mohammed by the angel Gabriel.

3. It is written in an Arabic style, which is perfect and unapproachable. "The best of Arab writers has never succeeded in producing its equal in merit."

4. Every syllable is of directly Divine origin. This includes the unintelligible combinations of letters put at the head of certain Suras.

5. Its text is incorruptible, "and preserved from error and variety of reading by the miraculous interposition of God Himself." To account, however, for the slight variants

* Muir, *Life of Mahomet*, p. 557.

which actually exist, the Koran is said to have been revealed in seven dialects.

6. As being the truth of God, it is the absolute authority, not only in religion and ethics, but also in law, science, and history.*

The point I make is : This is the kind of Bible we 'should like to have God give us, and when we construct for ourselves a theory of revelation we do it along these lines. Allow me to illustrate by a brief review of theories which have been held concerning the Old Testament. We naturally begin here with the Jew.

First, however, let us remark that the clear distinction which our theologians make between Revelation and Inspiration is a comparatively modern distinction. Inspiration naturally goes with Revelation. It is the Divine method of Revelation. A superintendence of the record as distinct from the giving of the truth did not occur to the ancients, because they did not reflect upon the record, except as containing the truth. Revelation and Inspiration, then, are not distinguished. The earliest Jewish testimonies concern themselves with the *Law* as contained in the book. This Law seems to be identified with the

* The authorities for these statements are, besides those already quoted, Nöldeke, *Geschichte des Qorans;* Hughes, *Dictionary of Islam;* Palmer, "The Qur'ân " (*Sacred Books of the East,* Vol. VI.).

heavenly Wisdom.* It is, therefore, as the Mohammedan would say, one of the attributes of God. When God would build the world, He looked upon the Tora as a builder looks upon the plan of a building.† This plan was delivered into the hands of Moses at Sinai by the angels in the form of a written book. This preference of the Law to the other Scriptures is very natural to the Jew, and its consequence is the distinction of two grades of inspiration. " Holy Scripture came into being by the inspiration of the Holy Spirit, and is therefore derived from God, who speaks therein. Nevertheless, there are within the Scripture different grades of Inspiration ; in that the Law is the primary revelation, the other Scriptures are secondary."

In inquiring into the history of this doctrine of Inspiration, we are struck, however, by the variety of opinion that has prevailed. Although the Jews give a higher place to the Law, yet at a later time they dignified the other books by making them also a part of the revelation to Moses. Rabbi Isaac said, " All that the prophets were to prophesy later they received from Mount Sinai, for so Moses declares,

---

* Sirach XXIV., 22. The reference to Baruch IV., 1, given by Weber, does not seem to assert the existence of the Law *from* eternity, though it asserts that it will endure for ever.

† Bereshith Rabba, I.

Deut. xxix. 15." * On the other hand, that Ezra may not be deprived of the glory belonging to him, later opinion made him the author of the whole Hebrew Bible, it having been lost during the captivity. So the Fourth Book of Esdras declares (xiv. 19-22) that the Law has been burned, and Ezra prays that it may be restored by him. God grants his desire, ordering him to provide five amanuenses. When he goes into the open country with the amanuenses, God gives him a cup to drink. When he has drunk he dictates to the scribes the twenty-four books of the Old Testament, and seventy others which he is ordered to keep secret. The fact that such various views could be held shows how impossible it is to speak of any established or settled view of Revelation or of Inspiration at this early time.

If we come down to the later period, however, we shall discover a theory of Inspiration which is definite enough, though it still refuses to distinguish Inspiration from Revelation. It starts with the Law as given at Mount Sinai. It identifies this with the received text of the punctuators. It affirms that even the form of the letters (*literæ finales, beth* at the beginning of Genesis) was ordained by God. "As Moses ascended the mountain he found God making the ornamental points [Ketharim] of

* Shemoth Rabba, XXVIII.

the letters [in the Law]." The extraordinary points, the Qeri and Kethibh, the division into paragraphs by spaces—these were all in the Divine model just as in a Hebrew Bible of the present day. Some scholars, however, were more radical and affirmed that the vowel points (and, of course, with them the sacred text) were given to Adam in Paradise. Others believed the points to have been added by Ezra and the so-called Great Synagogue. Mediating theologians tried to combine the different views. Azariah de Rossi supposed the points first communicated to Adam in Paradise and transmitted by him to Moses, to have been " partially forgotten, and their pronunciation vitiated during the Babylonian captivity ; that they had been restored by Ezra, but that they had been forgotten again in the wars and struggles during and after the destruction of the sacred Temple ; and that the Massorites, after the close of the Talmud, revised the system and permanently fixed the pronunciation by the contrivance of the present signs."*

To judge of the success of this author by general experience, we may conjecture that his well-meant attempt brought upon him the hatred of both parties. The general opinion of later Jewish authorities is to the effect that Ezra

* Ginsburg, *The Massoreth Ha-Massoreth of Elias Levita,* p. 53.

called a convention of elders and scribes on his return from the captivity—the prototype of the later Sanhedrim. This Great Synagogue first considered the subject of the Canon—gathering the sacred text into one volume and rejecting uninspired writings. They then deliberated on the text, marking off the verses, settling on the correct reading, the use of the vowel letters and the Qeri and Kethibh. They further added the points, both the vowel points and accents. As if this were not enough, they made also the Aramaic translations called the Targums, and added the Massora proper ; that is to say. they counted the number of letters, words and verses in each book, noted these figures in the margin, marked the middle word and verse in each book, and called special attention to unusual forms, that the scribes might make no mistake. This work, we may suppose, they stamped as authentic, and took measures to have it correctly transmitted.*

The influence of this theory upon Christian thinkers will be noticed later. The theory itself is certainly rigid enough, and its method would clearly secure an authentic Scripture. The only trouble with it is that it is entirely unsupported by facts. The Great Synagogue never had any existence. It has arisen from a misunderstanding of Ezra's activity in the

* Buxtorf, *Tiberias*, cc. X., XI. Schnedermann, *Die Controverse des L. Capellus mit den Buxtorfen u. s. w.*, p. 27.

great popular assembly, the account of which is contained in Nehemiah viii. Ezra's work at that time was, no doubt, of unspeakable moment. But in the account we have, it is a thoroughly practical one, instructing people in the Law and pledging them to its observance. Of settling the Canon we do not hear a word, and, indeed, we are tolerably certain that the whole Canon was not settled until a much later date. If Ezra (the Great Synagogue never existed, as I have said) did not even settle the Canon, much less can we suppose that he attended to the scrupulosities of the Massora. Concerning the vowel points, we know that they were not invented until somewhere near the eighth century of our era, and that the Massora is a growth of many centuries. Finally, the surprising uniformity of the Hebrew text has been secured by the loss or destruction of all copies that differed from one authorised model. But this model was settled upon certainly after the first Christian century.

We are discussing the subject of Inspiration, and it might seem at first sight as if all this Jewish theory was irrelevant. Let us notice, therefore, where we are. I suppose I am right in saying that we mean by Inspiration the Divine influence exerted upon the minds of the writers of the Bible, which led them to choose and shape their material so as to make the result

the authoritative rule of faith and practice
The Jewish theory concerning the Great
Synagogue was shaped by the same interest
which leads us to formulate a doctrine of
inspiration. And when Elias Levita showed
the late origin of the vowel points, he was
violently accused of what would be called
among us "low views of inspiration."

But I wish to go further, and as some
object to the assertion that such a thing as
bibliolatry is possible, to call your attention to
some other theories which have been held by
the Jews, and have also had large influence in
the Christian Church. The Jews were in
dead earnest when they argued that the Bible
is the Word of God, and therefore every item
in it is true. They went further, and concluded that every item in it is important truth
and worthy of God. In applying the theory
to the facts they would not be misled by
appearances. It does indeed seem that some
of the statements are trivial, and taken in
their literal sense they make difficulties. The
obvious conclusion is that they contain a
deeper sense. The search for this deeper
sense leads to the whole system of allegorical
interpretation of Scripture. Besides this, some
things in Scripture are ambiguous or obscure.
If we are to reach the truth we must have a
guide. The hypothesis of an inerrant Word
leads to the demand for an inerrant interpreta-

tion. The rabbinical authorities postulate both a deeper sense and an authoritative interpretation. The latter is provided in the so-called Oral Law, which, though embodied in comparatively late written documents, was held to be in fact as old as Moses, having been transmitted orally from him to the time of its written redaction, a period of about seventeen centuries. This view of the Mishna* (or even of the whole Talmud) has been maintained until comparatively recent times. "We cannot suppose that God would give an imperfect Law. An authorised interpretation is therefore needed, which we have in the Talmud (Oral Law). It is natural, therefore, that we [Jews] hold to this that we may not grope in darkness."† This view is even now the view of orthodox Judaism, and it is in substance as old as the New Testament. For we see that at that time the "traditions of the elders" had usurped the place of the Divine Law. It could hardly be otherwise. The Oral Law, as the alleged interpretation of the written command, must be immediately obeyed—it was itself the medium through which the written Law was obeyed. The simple Word was insufficient, while the traditional decision exactly met the particular need. The latter

* Gfrörer, I., 250 ; Weber, 87 ; Jost, *Geschichte des Judentums, I.,* 93.

† *Vide* A. T. Hartmann, *Die enge Verbindung des A.T. mit dem N.Y.,* p. 514.

was therefore the more important. This is
declared by a recent Jewish authority to be
" a universally recognised principle : *the decisions of the Scribes are more weighty than
those of the Law.*" The logical result, therefore, of this theory of inerrancy was to sub-
stitute for the Scripture the alleged authorised
interpretation.

The decisions of the wise, however, were
concerned with practical matters, points of
casuistry, such as always arise under a code of
morals. On the other side, much even of the
Tora is not embraced under the head of command or prohibition. To make use of this,
the system of allegory was developed. " The
fondness of the Jews for allegorical exposition
found its support in the belief that the excellence of the Tora lay in the inexhaustible
spring of varied interpretations indicated in
the assertion that the revelation was first
given in seventy languages. This variety was
deduced from Jeremiah xxiii. 29 : ' My words
are as a fire and as a hammer that breaks the
rock in pieces.' Who can count the fragments
into which the stone is shattered by a strong
arm, and who can count the sparks sent forth
by the fire ? "* Besides the theory that each
passage has seventy meanings, we hear that

* Hartmann, 534, quoting from Rashi on Gen. xxxiii. 20,
and Ex. vi. 11. The same in substance from the Talmud,
Weber 84.

Moses himself expounded each section in forty-nine different ways. This delirium reaches its height in the later assertion which makes each verse of the Law to contain no less than six hundred thousand meanings, if we may trust the authority of Eisenmenger. * But not to insist upon this, the methods of obtaining some of the admitted seventy meanings are calculated to show the small value of such a theory. One of these methods is the so-called Gematria, based on the numerical value of the letters. This value was calculated for any word, and the resulting number was put into the place of the word, or if this gave no sense any other word whose component letters gave the same sum might be substituted in its place. The numerical value of a single letter might be significant. The large ע (= 70) in Deut. vi. 4, is one of the arguments for the theory of seventy senses just considered. The letters might be interchanged by Athbash or Albam. †
A word might be taken as the basis of an acrostic, each of its letters taken as the initial of a new word, or it might be made into another by an anagram. In this way, from the first word of Genesis it was discovered

* Eisenmenger, *Entdecktes Judenthum*, I., 458.

† A for Z, B for Y, and so on, would represent the Athbash in English. A for N, B for O, and so on, the Albam.

that the world was created on a New
Year's Day,* and a word in Gen. ii. 4 shows
that the earth was created *for the sake of
Abraham.*

It is clear that this is simply exegetical
legerdemain, and it need not detain us
longer. Its main value is that it shows where
a high theory of the value of Revelation may
land us. It is in line with the declaration
of the Rabbis that God Himself studies the
Law three hours every day.† It brings with
it almost inevitably the magical application of
Scripture exemplified in the use of its verses as
charms or amulets, in regard to which we may
be pardoned for asserting that they have no
more real efficiency than a leaf from the mass-
book. But these extravagances aside, the
more sober form of the theory carried out in
the *allegorical* interpretation of Scripture has
been so important in the history of the Church
that we may profitably look at it a little more
closely. The most prominent exponent of it
among the Jews was Philo of Alexandria, and
his influence in the early Church can scarcely
be estimated. As a devout Jew, Philo accepted
the Old Testament as the Word of God, whose
inspiration extended to the most minute particulars, placing the highest value upon the
Law as he put Moses above the other pro-

* Reuss, 721; Buxtorf, *Tiberias* (1620), p. 163.
† Weber, p. 17.

phets. He does not confine his theory to the Hebrew text, but extends it to the Greek translators. "He accepts the story which ascribes to the translators of the Pentateuch a miraculous concurrence in the choice of words. He speaks of the translators themselves as 'hierophants and prophets,' and maintains that the Hebrew and Greek Scriptures are such that they must be admired and reverenced 'as sisters, or rather, as one and the same both in the facts and in the words.' He fully acts upon this belief, and . . . accords to the Greek text as profound a veneration and faith as if it had been written by the finger of God Himself."* On this basis Philo proceeds to discover the hidden truth by means of the allegorical method. All true wisdom is contained in this reservoir. Consequently, the Greek philosophy must have been derived from it. And the results obtained by his method are really those of Greek philosophy. His general system we may pass by for the present. What interests us is his theory of interpretation. This is that each verse of Scripture has, besides its natural grammatical or literal meaning, a secondary or higher sense.† This latter is the more

---

* Drummond, *Philo*, I., 15.

† This theory was not, of course, original with Philo, but already in use.—Schürer, *Geschichte des Jüdischen Volkes*, II., 871 ; Hartmann, 536.

important—the reality of which the literal
sense is only the shadow. To show what
he means, let me quote the following : " The
paradise in Eden is the type of virtue. The
stream which waters it is Goodness, which
divides into the four streams of the four
cardinal virtues."* Again, "the five cities
of the Plain destroyed by the Divine punishment for the abominations of their inhabitants,
are the five senses, the instruments of sinful
pleasure." The four ingredients of the incense
(Exod. xxx. 33) represent the four natural
elements. The incense itself ascending to God
represents the adoration of the universe made
up of these elements. In the great allegorical
commentary to Genesis, " the leading thought
is that the history of mankind as related in
Genesis is, in fact, an imposing psychology
and ethic. The different men described (good
and bad) are the different conditions of the
soul."† Astonishing as this appears to us,
there can be no doubt that it was employed
in all seriousness by a devout and profound
thinker, who supposed he was engaged in
developing the meaning of the Word as intended by God Himself. And it concerns us
here to notice that this method of exegesis was
compelled by the rigidity of the theory in connection with the nature of the facts of the

* Hartmann, 579.   † Schürer, II., 839.

record. The difficulty of interpreting the language of Scripture literally was such that the exegete took refuge in the higher sense. The theory of the later Rabbis, that the sacred text "could contain nothing derogatory to the Deity, and that it could contain nothing contrary to sound reason," was Philo's also. "Adam and Eve could not have hidden themselves from God, for God has interpenetrated the universe and left nothing empty of Himself; and, therefore, the account refers only to the false conception of the wicked man. . . . To suppose that God really planted fruit trees in Paradise when no one was allowed to live there, and when it would be impious to fancy that He required them for Himself, is 'a great and incurable silliness.' The reference, therefore, must be to the paradise of virtues with their appropriate actions implanted by God in the soul." * One is tempted to quote more at length, but these examples are sufficient to show how the allegorical sense must, under the claim of doing the highest honour to the Word of God, really nullify its natural and legitimate meaning.

From Philo the transition is natural to the Christian Church, in which, indeed, Philo was honoured almost as one of the Fathers. Before, however, we inquire into methods of inter-

---

* Drummond, I., 19.

pretation, let us notice the significant fact, that no one of the œcumenical councils of the undivided Church makes faith in the Scriptures a test of orthodoxy. Belief in the "Holy Ghost who spake by the prophets" is professed in one early creed; but the indefiniteness of the expression shows how little need was felt of a definition as to the nature of the written Word. It was after the middle of the fourth century before the Church felt the need of officially defining even the extent of the Canon, and this was done in provincial synods only, and the Apocrypha were included in the Old Testament. In fact, as has been said, "it did not at all seem at first as though Christ would found His Church upon a Scripture, or even as though the elaboration of a sacred record were an essential feature of its foundation."* The Church was, in fact, founded upon the spoken words of the Apostles, and after the Apostles had been removed from their earthly activity the tradition of their words was distinct enough to serve as a guide. But, of course, the Old Testament had its place as a means of instruction, and with it the method of instruction illustrated in Philo. The Epistle of Barnabas discovered in the three hundred and eighteen servants of Abra-

* Thiersch quoted by Dietzsch. *Studien und Kritiken* (1869), p. 472.

ham a prediction of the crucified Jesus.* The
method reminds us of the Gematria of the
Jews. Clemens of Alexandria sees in the
four colours of the Tabernacle the four natural
elements. Abraham's three days' journey to
the place of Moriah represents the three
stages of development of the human soul.
This author, indeed, says in so many words
that the whole Scripture has only allegorical
sense. †

Origen, the most learned man of the time,
perhaps the most learned man of antiquity,
adopts this theory to the full. He distinguishes a twofold or threefold sense, and values
the allegorical exposition because the simple
grammatical meaning of many passages is incredible or unworthy of God. The Latin
Fathers accepted the same theory. Ambrose
speaks of a threefold sense—historical (literal),
mystical, and moral. If the literal sense gives
us a contradiction, the solution is found in the
other senses. Augustine's generally sober judgment follows the same path, though his alle-
gories are rather types. Esau and Jacob are
types of Jew and Christian. Abel represents
the slain Christ, Seth the risen Christ, Joseph
the ascended Christ. Ham is "the sly generation of the heretics." Isaac, blind in his

---

* Diestel, *Geschichte des Alten Testamentes in der Christ-
lichen Kirche,* p. 31.

† Hartmann, p. 558.

old age, prefigures the blindness of the Jews.
The rock twice smitten with the rod points
to the cross of Christ, because two pieces of
wood [rods] joined together make a cross.
Even Jerome, whose work as translator made
him especially sensitive to the literal meaning,
follows the allegorical method in his exposition.
At the same time, he confesses that many difficulties are to him insoluble. It is of no use to
puzzle ourselves too much with the literal
sense, for the letter killeth.   In the chronology, especially, he finds such discrepancies
and confusion that he leaves the subject to the
dilettanti.*

These examples will suffice to show that
the Church before the Reformation had no
apprehension of the problem before us. In
a general way, Inspiration was held as connected with Revelation. But it was attributed
to the Apocrypha of the Old Testament as
well as to the canonical books. It was,
indeed, attributed to many pseudepigrapha
and even to heathen poets and philoso-
phers. But Apostolic tradition at first, and
afterwards the voice of the Church, was regarded as equally inspired, and this tradition
furnished the authority in faith and morals
upon which all men leaned. And when the
difficulties of the Scripture record forced

* Diestel, pp. 89 and 98.

themselves upon the careful student, they were explained by a supposed mystical or spiritual sense. In the Middle Age, the line was not sharply drawn between Scripture and the Fathers. Hugo of St. Victor, who is more reserved than many others, ranks as authorities (1) the Gospels, (2) the other books of Scripture, (3) the decretals and canons of the Church, (4) the writings of the Fathers. The latter contain the same truth with the others, only more clear and more expanded.* The Roman Catholic Church stands on this ground to-day. The Council of Trent formally asserts that it receives and venerates with equal piety and reverence all the books of the Old and New Testaments, *as also* the traditions dictated by Christ's own word of mouth, or by the Holy Ghost, and preserved in the Catholic Church by a continuous succession. Recent publications show that this church also holds in substance to the allegorical method of exposition. I will simply call attention here to some examples which have fallen under my eye: Eve is a type of the Virgin Mary. Sarah is a type of wisdom and virtue, and Hagar a type of philosophy, the handmaid of theology. Keturah's descendants represent the heretical sects of New Testament times. Abraham seeking a

---

* Diestel, p. 178.

bride for his son is a type of God the Father, who also seeks a bride (the Church) for His Son. Eliezer, who is sent on this errand, is the representative of the twelve Apostles. The well at which Rebecca is found corresponds to the water of baptism, and the presents brought by Eliezer are the Divine Word and the good works of the saints. Jacob's words, " I am Esau, thy firstborn," cannot be called a lie—they are a *mysterium*— in a tropical sense they are true. Jacob, in using them, is a type of the Gentiles, who claim and receive the adoption and blessing belonging to the Jewish people. Jacob had two wives. So Christ calls the Jew and the Gentile. Leah, the tender-eyed, is the blinded Israel. Pharaoh, who commanded the mid-wives to kill the Hebrew babes, is a type of Satan, who tries to destroy the virtues by means of human science and wisdom, which often lead to heresies. Deborah (the Syna-gogue) incites Barak (Israel) to battle against Sisera (Satan) and routs his forces. Jael (the Church) meets him, stupefies him with milk (prayer), and slays him with the nail (of the Cross). Samson even is made a type of Christ. Now, these examples are taken from a book published with the approval of Roman Catholic authorities * within the last ten years,

* Zschokke, *Biblische Frauen des Alten Testamentes*, Freiburg, 1882.

and written by a professor of theology in a distinguished university. They show with perfect clearness how the lofty profession of finding all truth in the Bible really unfits one to discover the real truth of the Bible. It is this virtual nullifying of Scripture by tradition against which the Protestant Church protests. To this church we now turn our attention.

The principle of the Reformation, I need not remind you, is a double one. Its two parts are justification by faith and the authority of Scripture alone in matters of faith and life. Of these two the former is the vital principle, the second is regulative. In Luther's own experience they developed in this order. He first experienced justification by faith. In order to maintain his Christian life, he had to defend it against the champions of the Church. At first he supposed he had also the authority of the Church on his side. But investigation showed him that this authority was at least divided. In this way he was driven back upon Scripture alone. Luther's theory was in substance this : Christ is presented to the sinner in the Gospel either as heard in the Church or as read in the Bible. He is immediately recognised as the needed Saviour and as the Son of God. He is appropriated by faith, and the believer is justified and adopted into the family of God. Up to

this point it is clear that nothing more is
claimed for the written Word than that it
gives a historically credible account of the life
of Christ. The peculiar normative quality of
the Word comes out in the subsequent life of
the believer and the Church. Questions of
doctrine and of duty arise. There will be
perplexities in the individual heart as well as
differences between different members of the
Church. To settle these the appeal is to the
written Word. It is clear that Luther would
claim no further infallibility for the Bible than
this, and, indeed, he expressly declares as much
in his judgment of the canon. He proposes
this rule : What proclaims Christ is Scripture. " What does not proclaim Christ is
not apostolic, though written by St. Peter or
by St. Paul. What proclaims Christ is apostolic,
though it were written by Judas, Annas, Pilate,
or Herod." On this internal evidence he would
include the first book of Maccabees in the
canon, as he would exclude the epistle of
James. He cannot bear the book of Esther
because it Judaises so. In regard to the
epistle to the Hebrews, he takes the middle
ground : "Although the author does not lay
the foundation of faith, which is the Apostle's
work, yet he builds thereon gold, silver, and
precious stones, as St. Paul says. If now some
wood, hay, or stubble is intermixed, this shall
not hinder our receiving the precious doctrine

with all honour—nevertheless, we may not make this equal to the apostolic epistles."* It is quite in accordance with this, that the first doctrinal treatise of the Reformation—Melanchthon's Loci—had no section on the doctrine of Scripture at all, while even in the later editions he only treats briefly the difference between the Old Testament and the New.† The early Swiss reformers stand on the same ground. "The Word of God *in Christ* is the highest authority. Zwingli finds church councils enough in the words of Christ." Bullinger says, in one instance, that the writers of the Bible are sometimes led astray by defective memory.‡ Calvin, as we might expect, is more full on the doctrine of Scripture, yet he does not give a clear statement as to the connection of inerrancy and inspiration, and, in fact, recognises the difficulties in the case. He does not hesitate to affirm that the Scriptures are written in "a humble and contemptible style." Three evangelists (he adds later) "recite their history in a low and mean style. Many proud men are disgusted with that simplicity, because they attend not to the principal points of doctrine."§ In his commentaries

* Luther, *Vorreden zur Heiligen Schrift.*
† Klaiber in the *Jahrb. f. Deutsche Theol.* II., p. 3.
‡ Quoted by Tholuck, *Zeitschr. fur Christl, Wissenschaft,* I., 139.
§ *Institutes,* I., VIII., X., and XI.

he concedes minor errors and discrepancies of the writers (compare Tholuck, p. 131). What Calvin emphasizes, in full accord with Luther, is the testimony of the Holy Spirit. " The testimony of the Spirit is superior to all reason [*i.e.*, to the Evidences usually adduced for Scripture]. For as God alone is a sufficient witness of Himself in His own Word, so also the Word will never gain credit in the hearts of men till it be confirmed by the internal testimony of the Spirit. It is necessary, therefore, that the same Spirit who spake by the mouths of the prophets should penetrate into our hearts to convince us that they faithfully delivered the oracles which were divinely entrusted to them. . . . Some good men are troubled that they are not always prepared with clear proof to oppose the impious when they murmur with impunity against the Divine Word, as though the Spirit were not, therefore, denominated a seal and an earnest for the confirmation of the faith of the pious ; because, till He illuminate their minds, they are perpetually fluctuating amidst a multitude of doubts. Let it be considered, then, as an undeniable truth, that they who have been inwardly taught by the Spirit, feel an entire acquiescence in the Scripture, and that it is self-authenticated, carrying with it its own evidence, and it ought not to be made the subject of demonstration and arguments from reason ;

but it obtains the credit which it deserves with us by the testimony of the Spirit." * There can be no doubt that these words of Calvin correctly state the position of the reformers. They are the source of the statements of the Protestant creeds on this subject, nearly all of which emphasize the testimony of the Holy Spirit, and no one of which ventures to affirm the inerrancy of Scripture apart from matters of faith and doctrine, unless it be the Swiss Formula Consensus, of which I shall speak later. † If. now, we ask, what it is that we are assured of by this testimony, we shall agree that it is the articles of sin and law and grace which Melanchthon makes the subjects of his Loci. Or, as the Heidelberg Catechism says: Three things are necessary for me to know: first, the greatness of my sin and misery; second, how I am redeemed from all my sins and misery; third, how I am to be thankful to God for such redemption. These are the things which the Holy Spirit sets before us in Scripture, and moved by that same Holy Spirit we recognise in the portraiture the Divine Author and accept the Word as His. "All in this Book is tributary to sin and salvation;

---

* *Institutes,* VII., IV. and V.

† The Irish Articles which, however, were soon superseded by the Thirty-nine Articles, affirm the Canonical Books to be of "most certain credit" as well as of the highest authority.

all leads up to Calvary." This I heard from one of our own pulpits, recently, and this is in harmony with the voice of the Evangelical Church in her creeds and confessions.

But because we recognise the Divine authorship of the doctrine set forth in the Bible, does it follow that we have a guarantee for every detail of its historical statement? Because you recognise the voice of God addressing you as a sinner, and freely inviting you to Christ, can you therefore assert, for example, that the list of Dukes of Edom, in Genesis (ch. xxxvi.), is exactly and absolutely correct? This is the question which confronts us when we come to make the Bible a historical study. It is evident that the great reformers would have answered the question in the negative, and they would have declared that whether this list were correct or not made no difference as to the main question. The following generation of theologians, however, did not so answer the question. From the inspiration of the Bible they deduced its historical accuracy on every point. The reasons for this are not far to seek. After the Council of Trent, the Roman Catholic polemic became sharper. It became the endeavour of the Roman Catholic party to show the necessity of tradition and the untrustworthiness of Scripture alone. This led the Protestants to defend the Bible more tenaciously than before. In addition, the scho-

lastic philosophy, though almost contemp-
tuously rejected by Luther, still influenced the
minds of men. The thick quartos of Gerhard,
as has been recently said, would lose a good
part of their dimensions were they deprived of
what was borrowed from Thomas Aquinas.
We are here concerned simply with the effect
of this movement upon the doctrine of Holy
Scripture. This doctrine was of course more
sharply formulated. It was extended to the
style of the writers. It affirmed that each book
of the Canon *must* have been formally approved
and joined to the others as soon as written. It
went great lengths in affirming the perspicuity
of Scripture, or if it admitted the difficulty of
some passages it explained them as God's
method of stimulating study by curiosity, or
even as the Divine arrangement for impressing
upon the laity due respect for the learning of
the ministry. Finally, the errorless transmission was made equally a matter of logical
deduction. That I may not be suspected of
exaggeration, let me give you a few details.
It was denied by Voetius " that any examination or reflection was necessary on the part of
the inspired writer in regard to that which was
written, since it was given him immediately
and in an extraordinary manner," * contra-
dicting Luke i. 1—4. Even the language and
style of the Bible must be wholly faultless.

* Van Oosterzee, *Dogmatics*, I., 171.

15

Diversity of style was denied or explained as a matter of Divine choice simply. "The Holy Spirit had a preference [*singularem gustum*] for the style of Polybius; therefore he chose this among all then existing Greek styles." *
Quotations already made show how much more correct was Calvin's view. "Whatever is related by the Holy Scriptures is absolutely true [*verissima*], whether it pertains to doctrine, morals, history, chronology, topography, or nomenclature; and there can be, there must be, no ignorance, carelessness or forgetfulness attributed to the amanuenses of the Holy Spirit in writing the sacred books." † The consequence is drawn with rigour—there can be no error in the transmission, no more than in the original. For where would be the certainty or truth of Scripture were there any errors of transmission? So far we have been describing the Lutheran view. The same tendency is visible in the Reformed Church. But it is worth noting that this period of stringent devotion to the infallibility of Scripture is the period of the bitterest polemic among the Protestant Churches. Calovius, the most consistent upholder of this doctrine of Inspiration, was one of the bitterest enemies of the Cal-

---

* Calovius, quoted by Klaiber, *Zeitsch. Luther. Theol.*, 1864, 23.

† Quenstedt, quoted by Luthardt, *Compendium der Dogmatik*, p. 294.

vinists, hated them worse than he did the Roman Catholics, used his influence to put them down by the civil power, and attacked with all the virulence of a strong and uncompromising nature Calixtus, who tried to find a *modus vivendi* with the other churches. Nor should we forget here that this was the century in which the Copernican system triumphed in astronomy, and that among its opponents were found these theologians who opposed to it indubitable proofs from Scripture.* In the Reformed Churches there was the same tendency to emphasize the Divine factor in Inspiration. The influence of the two Buxtorfs in the Swiss Churches led to an especial emphasis on the Jewish theories of the Old Testament Canon. It was held that the Canon was settled by the Great Synagogue, and that the points were a part of the revelation to Ezra, from whom also the Massora was derived.

The ascription of the points to Adam even was revived by some zealous theologians. The younger Buxtorf found it difficult to decide between Adam, Moses, and Ezra as the original punctuator. The discussion of this point led to the adoption of the Swiss Formula Consensus, in 1675, which declared the vowel points to be inspired. This is the only Protestant creed, however, which took

---

* So Calovius and Voetius, cf. *Gass*, pp. 342, 461.

such a stand, and it was of only local importance, and even in Switzerland it had but temporary validity.   It is evident, then, that these
high and stringent theories were never the
theories of the Church.   In fact, there never
were lacking men in the Evangelical churches
who protested against them or refused to
accept them.   The history of the doctrine of
the Hebrew vowel points is instructive in this
regard, and for this reason I venture to call
attention to it somewhat more at length.

As there may be some laymen interested in
this matter, let me explain that the letters
of the Hebrew alphabet are, in their original
force, all consonants.   The vowels are supplied
by smaller signs, called points, placed in, over,
or beneath the letters.   The three letters k, t, l,
may represent, therefore, a number of different
forms, as katal, kittel, kotel, kuttal.   In practice, however, the context is nearly always
sufficient to decide what word is intended in
a particular place, and no difficulty is felt by
the practised scholar in reading unpointed
texts, and these are in use in all Hebrew
books except the Bible.   For the sake of
accuracy, however, the Bible is generally
written (and printed) with the points.   As
we have seen, the later Jewish theory ascribes
these points to Ezra, if not to Moses or Adam;
and this opinion was embraced by the Buxtorfs and others, who felt that God could not

have committed His Word to an uncertain script. The attack on this view was made about the same time by two men. One of them, Morinus, was a Roman Catholic, and he was (at least) partially moved by a desire to overthrow the security of the Protestants, and to prove the necessity of the tradition of the Church, in order to a correct interpretation of the Bible. But he called attention to facts overlooked by the Protestants, and so far forth aided to a correct solution of the problem—eventually, that is, for his polemic tone hindered at first a correct estimate of his arguments. The other champion of the late origin of the points was Lodovicus Cappellus, Professor in the French Protestant College at Saumur. He was at first, as he avows, of the opinion of Buxtorf. Against his will, he was forced, by facts, to the opposite conclusion. His observations were embodied in a treatise,* the MS. of which was sent to Buxtorf the elder for his opinion. As this distinguished scholar advised against the publication, Cappellus sent the manuscript to Erpenius, a distinguished Dutch orientalist, and Erpenius published it at once, with a preface of his own, but without the author's name. The history of the younger Buxtorf's attack and

---

* *Arcanum Punctationis Revelatum.* Republished in one volume, folio, with the *Notæ Criticæ and the Vindiciæ Arcani,* 1689.

Cappellus's rejoinder need not be given in detail. But we may learn something from the method of argument pursued. It is, on Cappellus's side, partly a careful examination of the reasons adduced by the advocates of antiquity, partly the marshalling of facts by them overlooked or not allowed due weight. For example, it had been alleged that the points are necessary to the correct understanding of the text. But this is by no means so. Modern Hebrew, as well as Syriac and Arabic, are constantly read and printed without points, and no difficulty is felt in reading and understanding them by those familiar with the languages. Again, the opinion of the Jews had been alleged. But this is by no means unanimous, and in fact the weight of authority is rather against the antiquity than for it. Elias Levita, himself no mean scholar, was sustained by Kimchi and other distinguished authorities. And among the authorities cited by Buxtorf some were certainly of very recent date. So far the reply to allegations. Now positive arguments are the following: first, the argument from silence. The points are not mentioned by Jerome or by the Talmud. Buxtorf might reply, indeed, "They may have existed, nevertheless." And, indeed, the silence of an author concerning a fact may not prove the non-existence of the fact. But in some circumstances the argument from silence is very weighty indeed. Jerome had frequent occasion to discuss points of Hebrew grammar. He mentions the letters and their occasional ambiguity. Had the points existed, he would surely have mentioned them; and so of the Talmud, which often discusses the different possible meanings of Bible verses. Again, the fact that the Jews use an unpointed roll of the Law in the synagogue shows that the points are not ancient. Ecclesiastical customs, as we know, are conservative—tenacious of old forms. Had the points been introduced by Ezra they would have been introduced everywhere. The unpointed synagogue rolls are survivals of ancient custom. Another argument is the complication of the system itself. It is entirely too elaborate to be the invention of a single age; it bears all the marks of having grown up through several generations. To all these arguments Buxtorf can only reply by hypotheses, designed to admit what he was compelled to admit, but at the same time to show how his theory might be held, nevertheless. His main argument was the danger to the Christian faith of the new hypothesis.

As I have said, it is now known as definitely as any historic facts can be known that Cappellus was right. The points were not invented until after the redaction of the Talmud, and they were then gradually developed through two or three centuries. The reasons which establish this fact are those urged by Cappellus himself. Notice, they are *critical* reasons, mainly belonging to what we now know as the lower criticism to be sure, but critical, nevertheless. And, indeed, it is often difficult to draw the line between the lower criticism and the higher. Criticism is simply the careful examination of the facts to discover what they really teach. It takes no assertions without examining the grounds on which they are made. And having carefully examined the facts, it seeks for the hypothesis which will most naturally explain them all.

The point we have reached is the high-water mark of the doctrine of Inspiration. We have discovered that the early Church had no doctrine of Inspiration in our sense of the word Inspiration. Its affirmations are invalidated by a theory of allegory, which completely overshadows and destroys the true sense of Scripture. The reformers who swept this away were concerned with the testimony of the Holy Spirit, which assures us of matters of doctrine and duty in the Word of God, with no interest in affirming historic inerrancy. The extreme development of Protestant dogmatics in the seventeenth century, in opposition to the Roman Catholic polemic, led to unwarranted emphasis of the Divine side of

Scripture, and an almost total ignoring of the human side. This theology, in strict logic, as it supposed, affirmed the perfection of style of the Bible, its freedom from grammatical errors, the absence from it of accommodation to human limitations, its strict accuracy even in the matter of natural science, topography, and chronology, and, finally, its miraculous preservation from transmissional corruption by means of the Massoretic system.* The majority of these points are now universally given up.

It is of more importance to note that this extreme theory was always the theory of some theologians only. There always were evangelical and devout men who did not accept it. But that I may not weary you with historical details, let me come down to the practical point of the teaching of to-day. I shall probably not be wrong in assuming that so much of the theory of verbal inerrancy as can be held at the present day is held, stated, and defended by Prof. Gaussen, late of Geneva, whose book on Inspiration† has in our theological world almost the dignity of a classic. I will endeavour to state his theory.

---

* No one seems to have been staggered by the fact that the Old Testament alone received such a remarkable system for its preservation.

† *Theopneusty, or the Plenary Inspiration of the Holy Scriptures.* Translated by E. N. Kirk. New York, 1842.

Prof. Gaussen states his case in this way (p. 40): "The Scriptures are given and guaranteed by God even in their very language." As an alternative statement of the same thing he gives: "The Scriptures contain *no error;* that is, they say all they ought to say, and only what they ought to say.' You will notice that the point upon which the whole theory turns is the definition of the word *error.* It is clear that the author means error of any kind, for later he admits "that if it be true that there are, as is said, erroneous statements and contradictory accounts in the Holy Scriptures, their plenary inspiration must be renounced " (p. 110). The alleged errors which he discusses under this head, and the existence of which he denies, are: discrepancies in the Gospel narrative, points of chronology, and matters of physical science. In regard to the last named, he says: "We freely admit that if there are any physical errors fully proved in the Scriptures, the Scriptures could not be from God. But we mean to show there are none, and we shall dare to challenge the adversaries to produce one from the entire Bible.' He then proceeds to show the accuracy of the expression in Joshua, "The sun stood still in the midst of heaven." There is, then, he says, "no physical error in Scripture, and this great fact, which becomes more admirable in proportion as it is more closely contemplated, is a striking proof of the inspiration which has dictated to their writers even in the choice of the least expression." There would seem to be no doubt, therefore, of the meaning of this author. I have always supposed Dr. Charles Hodge to mean the same thing when he says (Theol., I., 152) that the Scriptures are " free from all error, whether of doctrine, fact, or precept." If what the sacred writers assert, he says later (p. 163), *God* asserts, which, as has been shown, is the Scriptural idea of inspiration, their assertions must be free from error." Again, he says, " The whole Bible was written under such an influence as preserved its human authors *from all error*, and makes it for the Church the infallible rule of faith and practice." Notice there are two statements here. Had Dr. Hodge contented himself with affirming that the whole Bible was written " under such an influence as makes it for the Church the infallible rule of faith and practice," no one could have objected. The other clause is the one to which we object, and whose application to the Old Testament I affirm to be impossible. Drs. Hodge and Warfield, in their well-known article, say: " It is evident, therefore, that every supposed conclusion of critical investigation which denies the apostolic origin of a New Testament book, or the truth of any part of Christ's testimony in relation to the Old Testament and its contents, *or which is inconsistent with the absolute truthfulness of any affirmation* of any book so authenticated, must be inconsistent with the true doctrine of inspiration ; " and again : " The historical faith of the Church has always been that *all affirmations of Scripture of all kinds,* whether of spiritual doctrine or duty, or of physical or historical fact, or of psychological or philosophical principle, are *without any error* when the *ipsissima verba* of the original autographs are ascertained and interpreted in their natural and intended sense." * These statements are exactly in line with those of the authors quoted above, except that they make a reservation concerning the transmission of the documents. Now, these authors (p. 237) admit that this statement is to be tried by the facts, and it is to the facts of the Old Testament that I propose to go. First, however, allow me a word of personal explanation. Some years ago, when a candidate for ordination, I received as a text for my trial sermon the well-known passage of II. Timothy, " All Scripture is given by inspiration of God." In that sermon I took the very ground of the authors I have been quoting.

* *Presbyterian Review,* 1881, pp. 236 and 238. The italics are mine.

For more than fifteen years since that time I have been engaged in the direct daily study of the Old Testament. It has been my duty to familiarise myself with the facts of the record, and as well with the statements of scholars about those facts. I well recall the reluctance which I felt to read some books which departed from "the views commonly received among us," and on reflection I cannot convict myself of undue sympathy with German mysticism or rationalism. But I have felt it my duty to know facts, and I sincerely believe that the truth of God is evident in all the facts of His Word. But in the examination of facts to which I now proceed, remember that it is my desire to give no one pain. And I ask you not to take my statement, but to examine the record itself. Dr. Charles Hodge well says (I. p. 11): "Almost all false theories in science and false doctrines in theology are due in a great degree to mistakes as to matters of fact." Three classes of facts seem to have been ignored by the advocates of an in-errant Inspiration.

1. The first class is the least important, and may be said not to bear upon inerrancy. It includes the cases where writings have been included in the books of those who were not their authors. I will not take up the Pentateuch which has recently been discussed at length by others. The hypothesis

of a redactor there has met with so little favour that it may be well to strengthen his position by showing his activity elsewhere. Look first at the Minor Prophets. We have them, as you know, in twelve separate books. They are, however, in the Hebrew Bible one book. It is clear that an editor has gathered together what prophetic fragments were in circulation in his time and united them in one roll. His activity was confined to arranging them in order. He may have added the titles in some cases, but his knowledge of the authors was slight. That Joel was the son of Pethuel; that one fragment was a vision of Obadiah, and that one contained the word of the Lord to Israel by Malachi—these are very slight additions to our knowledge. Suppose, now, he found a fragment without the author's name and inserted it in the series. It would not have been distinguished externally from the work of the author immediately preceding. This is what the critics suppose actually to have taken place. In the book assigned to Zechariah there is a sharp distinction in style and situation between the first eight chapters and the rest of the book. The second half is assigned to an older prophet. Strictly speaking, the hypothesis does not contradict the doctrine of inerrancy, and I should not have alluded to it except to prepare the way for a similar case which has made no small scandal in the theological world. I allude, of course, to the book of Isaiah. Divest your mind of preconceptions now, and look at this case. Let us suppose the redactor of the book of the Minor Prophets to have had a book of Isaiah which included only the first thirty-nine chapters of our book of that name. He has also in his possession the magnificent evangelical prophecy which is more familiar to us than almost any other part of the Old Testament. He does not know the author's name, or perhaps it is not safe to have it known. What more likely than that he should make it an appendix to the book of the kindred prophet—the two together make up a roll about the size of the book of the Twelve. This would not be out of harmony with the process of gathering the other book, and the only way in which it would violate the strictest theory of inspiration is in making appear as Isaiah's what is not his. But it will be replied, as has so often been replied: this is a merely gratuitous hypothesis, one of those wild vagaries of the German seekers after novelty of which we have had so many. Let us look, therefore, at the arguments by which the critics support their vagary.

In the first place, it is known that the earliest order of the prophetical books in the Old Testament Canon was Jeremiah, then Ezekiel, then

Isaiah. The only reason for departing from the chronological order that can be suggested is that the Book of Isaiah was felt to be an anthology like that of the Minor Prophets.

Secondly, it is rather curious that a narrative piece (chapters xxxvi.-xxxix.) should be found in the middle of the Book of Isaiah. Such a notice would come more naturally at the close of the book. We actually find one at the end of Jeremiah. There is nothing extravagant in the supposition, therefore, that the redactor of Isaiah's works had concluded his book with this historical notice, and that the last twenty-seven chapters were added to a book already complete.

The third argument, from style, is of course less obvious to the English reader; but I think even the English reader will discover differences.

Lastly, the situation in the second part of the book is entirely different from that in the first part. Read over the first chapter of Isaiah as a characteristic sermon of the prophet. Note the commanding tone in which he calls heaven and earth to hear his arraignment of Israel. Look at the Israel he depicts in its pride, and sinfulness and hypocrisy. " Hear the word of Jehovah, rulers of Sodom ! Give ear to the instruction of our God, people of Gomorrha ! To what purpose is the multitude of your sacrifices, saith Jehovah ? I am

sated with holocausts of rams and the fat of
fatlings ; and the blood of bulls and lambs and
goats I do not delight in. When ye come to
see my face—who hath required this at your
hands, to trample my courts? Bring no more
vain oblations; incense is an abomination to
me; new moon and Sabbath, the calling of
assembly—I cannot abide iniquity with festive
meeting." Now, after reading this chapter,
turn to the fortieth : " Comfort ye, comfort ye,
my people, saith your Lord! Speak to the
heart of Jerusalem, and cry unto her that her
term of service is completed, that her guilt is
pardoned, that she hath received of the hand of
Jehovah double for all her sins. Hark! One
cries in the wilderness : Prepare the way of
Jehovah, level in the desert a highway for our
God. Every valley shall be filled up and every
mountain and hill brought low, and the steep
shall be made level, and the rough country a
valley. And the glory of Jehovah shall be
revealed, and all flesh shall see it, for the
mouth of Jehovah has spoken." Now, what I
say is : Read through this whole second part.
Note how God comforts His mourning people,
promises to deliver them, speaks to Zion as
desolate and forsaken, a captive and an outcast,
promises to bring back her children, to rebuild
her walls, to punish her oppressors. Read this,
and you will feel that the message could have
come with appropriateness to the people in the

captivity, and not to the people of Isaiah's time, whose situation was so different. This is, at any rate, the conclusion of the majority of the critics. No one denies the genuineness of the prophecy; no one denies that it is a genuine prophecy, that is; and this being admitted, it gains in force and beauty on the critical theory.

Now, if we admit the critical conclusions in this case, the question is whether they affect the doctrine of inerrancy. I do not see that they do, that is to say, they do not show the inaccuracy of any *statement* of Scripture, though they show the inaccuracy of the arrangement of Scripture. I pass to a more serious case. As you are well aware, the Book of Psalms is generally ascribed to David. The reason is that a number of individual Psalms bear his name in the title. Probably, no one now goes to the length of some of the Rabbis and Fathers in supposing that David wrote the whole book. But, as in the original the titles form a part of the text, there has been a strong disposition among conservative commentators to vindicate *their* accuracy. But the critical conclusion is different in regard to a number of them. I will adduce only one, Psalm cxxxix., which is ascribed to David, both in the Hebrew and in the Seventy. But only a slight knowledge of the language is necessary to see that it is entirely different in

style from any other Psalm attributed to David.
The difference is not of a kind that exists between the various compositions of the same
man. The language is the language of another
epoch. If you were to find a poem of Burns
published in Shakespeare's works, you would
not suppose it Shakespeare's. Shakespeare is
versatile, to be sure. He could vary his style
to suit any exigency. But you know he never
wrote like Burns. Now this is not an exaggerated statement of the case with this
Psalm. I have one more instance under this
head—the Book of Ecclesiastes. As you are
already familiar with the problem, I will only say
that the postexilic authorship was announced
by Luther, and is accepted by as orthodox
scholars as Delitzsch and Ginsburg. In fact,
the argument is as strong as it can possibly be
from style and vocabulary. To suppose Solomon the author of the book is about like supposing Spenser to have written *In Memoriam.*
There can be no question, on the other side, that
the author assumes the character of Solomon.
So that we have a clear case of a sacred writer
writing under an assumed name. Many Bible
students see nothing improper in an inspired
writer using any form of literature, and after
Bunyan's immortal allegory, *fiction* would seem
not to be an unworthy vehicle of spiritual truth.
But if we admit this, then the theory, that every
statement of an inspired writer is without error

in its natural and legitimate sense cannot be maintained.

2. For my second class of facts, I will ask you to look at the historical books from Joshua to Kings, inclusive. We have here a series of books which give a connected narrative for the period from the conquest of Canaan to the Exile. Of course, it is conceivable that such a narrative should be made after the method of an official register. Each scribe would add to the book a sketch of his own time and pass it on to his successor. It has been supposed by some that the Hebrew records were kept in this way, but the theory is without support from the facts. The continuity of the narrative from Joshua to Zedekiah has been secured by editing. The method of the redactor is quite plain. He has made up his story by extracts from already existing documents, making very little change of himself, but inserting an occasional note which serves to make the connection clear. As he refers us to the Chronicles of the Kings of Judah (or Israel as the case may be), it is clear that one of his sources was an extensive historical work bearing this title. But the fact of compilation is clear in other places than those in which he mentions his authority. Take for example the Book of Judges. Chapter ii. 6, reads : " Now, when Joshua had sent the people away, the children of Israel went every

man unto his inheritance." Then follows the mention of the death and burial of Joshua. It is clear that this was originally the beginning of the book. And the book of which this was the beginning extended through chapter xvi. It was strictly a book of the Judges. Itself, however, was a compilation, as is evident from the varying character of its parts. This book, after it was finished, received two supplements: one, the story of Micah, the other, of the war against Benjamin. These belong chronologically at the beginning of the book, for one is dated when Jonathan, the son of Gershom, and therefore grandson of Moses, was still a young man, which could not have been long after the death of Joshua. In the other, Phinehas, the son of Eleazar, the son of Aaron, is High Priest, and this must have been about the same time. The book received also a preface, giving an account of the gradual conquest of the land. Let me call your attention to one section only of this preface. It is i. 10-15, and it contains the account of the conquest of Hebron by Caleb. The same account is contained in Joshua xv. 13-19. In one case Joshua gave Hebron to Caleb; in the other the children of Judah went against it "after the death of Joshua." It is clear that we have here an inaccuracy in one of the narratives. The difficulties in the history of David are well known. In one

chapter he is already a warrior when invited
to the court to play before Saul. Saul loves
him and makes him his armour-bearer. In the
other he is a stripling who comes providentially
into camp in time to meet the giant, and
appears to be wholly unknown to Saul. I
know the latter account is not in the Seventy
in the earliest form of that version. But this
only shows the extreme freedom with which
the text was treated at a very late date, and
even leaving out the part not in the Seventy,
we still have serious discrepancies.

It is not to emphasize these discrepancies
that I call attention to these facts at this point,
but to show the extreme difficulty of applying
the theory of inerrancy to documents of this
kind. The theory is that " all affirmations of
Scripture of all kinds are without any error."
Now, what are " the affirmations of Scripture "
in the cases we have been considering? The
theologians are careful to tell us that inerrancy
does not guarantee the truthfulness of the words
of Satan in Gen. iii., or of the speeches of Job's
friends in their argument with him.

What shall we say of the books we have
been discussing? Where is the point of inerrancy? Is it in the originals from which
the narrative has been compiled? Is it in
the arrangement? Is it in the notes of the
the redactor? Or is it in all these? Some
of the advocates of inerrancy have declined to

postulate inerrant transmission, because it would call for a standing miracle. The continuous influence which would secure original inerrancy for all the documents would be just such a standing miracle. The Song of Deborah was composed, let us say, 1,300 years B.C. The final touches to the books we are considering were given not earlier than the Exile, which began about 600 B.C. The materials which are now in our historical books, therefore, were composed during a period of seven hundred years. Was there a standing miracle during all this time? Or shall we assume that the final redactor received the gift of inerrancy so that he changed the language of his sources so as to leave no inaccuracies? Of this, again, there is no evidence. For, arguing on the basis of individual style, we discover that the redactor has generally left unaltered the documents he has embodied in his narrative. His supervision has generally gone only so far as to make an occasional note or insert a connecting phrase. Or does his inerrancy extend simply to the reproduction, so that our confidence extends only to the accuracy of his quotation? This, indeed, is what the critics generally accept. But it is far from what the advocates of inerrancy claim. Unless we can assume the standing miracle, the historical sources of the Old Testament need, in order to discover the truth of events, the same sort of analysis, sifting, and cross-questioning that must be given to other sources of history. And this analysis, sifting, and cross-questioning is precisely—higher criticism.

Before we leave this point, let us look at another phase of it. Several books of the Old Testament—notably the Psalms, Proverbs, Job, and Ecclesiastes—labour under the same difficulty of discovering where the statements of the author are—those statements which are free from error. Take the book of Job, for example. It presents us the picture of a grand trial. The pious sufferer has to contend with fears within as well as fightings without. It is not only the speeches of his friends which contain error, Job himself loses sight of God. He doubts His justice and His love. The author does not make his own opinion heard. He lets the situation speak to us. The value of the book lies not in any assertion even of God Himself—sublime as is the truth He speaks. No ; the value of the book of Job lies in the spectacle of a human soul in the direst affliction working through its doubts and at last humbly confessing its weakness and sinfulness in the presence of its Maker. The inerrancy is in the truth of the picture presented. It cannot be located in any statement of the author or of any of his characters. The same is true of the Psalms. They present us a picture of pious experience in all its phases. We see every variety of soul in every variety of emotion. The assertions of the authors cannot be taken for absolute truth. Nor can the authors, though doubtless all were sincere believers in God, be taken as sinless models for the Christian. Only Christ is that. The Psalms present us a record of actual experience of believers in the past. We can study and profit by this experience all the more that it has in it human weakness. The subjects of the experience doubtless had the power of correctly expressing their feelings, but that is not the inerrancy which has been claimed for them, and which the theologians desire. The imprecations which have been such a stumbling-block to some are enough to prove this point.

3. So far we have noticed the difficulty of applying the theory of inerrancy. We are in a position, however, to go further. We have, as you know, two parallel histories in the Old Testament. One is contained in the books from Genesis to 2 Kings; the other is contained in the books of Chronicles. These latter, indeed, once were joined with Ezra and Nehemiah, so as to form a continuous narrative (if narrative it may be called, where so much is simply genealogical) from Adam to the Persian monarchy. But this does not now concern us. For our present inquiry, we

are interested in the two forms of the history of Israel as presented on the one side in the books of Samuel and Kings, and on the other in the books of Chronicles. The study of these books shows the method of the authors with a definiteness which leaves nothing to be desired. We see that the Chronicler had before him our book of Kings as one of his sources. He takes from it what suits his purpose. What he takes he generally transfers without material change. He omits a good deal which does not answer his purpose, and he inserts a good deal from other sources. He pursues exactly the plan, that is, which we suppose to have been followed by the other historical writers. Now compare the following passages :—

2 Sam. viii. 4. And David took from him 1,700 horsemen and 20,000 footmen.

1 Chron. xviii. 3. And David took from him 1,000 chariots, and 7,000 horsemen, and 20,000 footmen.

x. 16. The children of Ammon sent and hired the Syrians of Beth Rehob and the Syrians of Zobah 20,000 footmen, and the King of Maacah with 1,000 men, and the men of Tob 1,200 men.

xxix. 6. Hanun and the children of Ammon sent 1,000 talents of silver to hire them chariots and horsemen. So they hired them 32,000 chariots and the King of Maacah and his men.

x. 18. David destroyed of the Syrians 700 chariots.

xix. 18. David destroyed of the Syrians 7,000 chariots.

xxiv. 9. There were in Israel 800,000 valiant men who drew sword, and the men of Judah were 500,000.

xxi. 5. There were of all Israel 1,100,000 that drew sword and Judah was 470,000 that drew sword.

xxxiv. 24. So David bought the threshing floor and the oxen for 50 shekels of silver.

xxi. 25. So David gave to Ornan for the place 600 shekels of gold by weight.

1 Kings iv. 26. And Solomon had 40,000 stalls for horses.

2 Chron. ix. 25. And Solomon had 4,000 stalls for horses and chariots.

xvi. 2. The height [of the house] 30 cubits.

iii. 4. The height [of the porch] 120 cubits.

vii. 26. It [the brazen sea] held 2,000 baths.

iv. 5. It received and held 3,000 baths.

Now, it will be said at once that these are all discrepancies in numbers which are very liable to corruption, and that therefore these are all cases of error in transmission. But I ask you to notice that these are, all but one, cases in which the larger number is in the text of the Chronicler. Where the age of a king or the length of his reign is concerned, I have not taken account of the difference. But in matters of statistics it is curious that the errors should be nearly all one way. Remembering that the Chronicler was much further away in time from the events narrated, we find it natural that he should have an exaggerated idea of the resources of his country in the days of her glory. In the case of David's purchase of the field of Ornan, he finds the price a

niggardly one for a prince to pay. He therefore does not hesitate (supposing that a mistake has been made) to put in a larger sum.
Of course, we need not lay this to the charge
of the final redactor of the book. He had
probably before him other written elaborations
of the history in which his exaggerated idea of
the past was already embodied. The personal
equation is as difficult to suppress in the
historian as is individuality of style. Why
should one be overruled any more than the
other? The Chronicler lived in a time when
the Mosaic law had taken substantially the
position we find it occupying in the New Testament times. Piety was to him the observance
of this law. He looked back through this
medium to David and Solomon and the good
kings of their line. He had lost all interest
in the Israel of the Ten Tribes, because they
had disappeared from his vision, or lived only
in the heretical Samaritans of his time. Now,
we all know how difficult it is to picture to
ourselves a different piety from our own.
Abraham, the Father of the Faithful, we picture to ourselves as an enlightened Christian of
the nineteenth century. We do not like to
confess that he was guilty of deception, or that
Jacob, the Prince of God, took an unfair
advantage of his own brother. So with the
Chronicler. He could think of David only
as a saint of his own pattern. Therefore, he

does not copy from the older history the shadows that rest upon David's life. His adultery, the trouble with Amnon, the usurpation of Absalom and of Adonijah, the charge of vengeance delivered to Solomon—these are left out of his history altogether. To him David is the nursing father of the legitimate priesthood, and the virtual builder of the Temple. But you will say this does not give us error in the record. Let me, then, call attention to the following :

1 Kings ix. 11. Solomon gave Hiram 30 cities in the land of Galilee.	2 Chron. viii. 2. The cities which Hiram gave Solomon, Solomon built them and caused the children of Israel to dwell there.
xv. 14. But the *high places* were not taken away. Nevertheless, the heart of Asa was perfect with the Lord all his days.	2 Chron. xiv. 3. For he took away the strange altars and the *high places* (cf. v. 5: Also he took away out of all the cities of Judah the high places).

These certainly look on their face like direct contradictions, and if we allow for the personal equation of which I have spoken, we can easily explain them. It would be hard indeed for a Jew of the Persian period to imagine Solomon giving away the sacred territory of Israel to the heathen king. Rather must he suppose the mighty Solomon to be the recipient of gifts of territory. The same line of reasoning is followed in the second quotation. The high places were the old sanctuaries of Jehovah, regarded as legitimate before the building of the Temple, even by the author of the book of Kings (1 Kings iii. 2), and used without reserve by Samuel. As time went on they fell more and more into disrepute, and after the exile the requirements of the law were carried out, and the only sanctuary of the people was the Temple at Jerusalem. The remembrance of the high places was only that of illegitimate places of worship. The Chronicler and his generation could not imagine a good king as even tolerating them. Hence the change in his account. Allow me to call your attention to one more instance. If you will compare the two accounts of the coronation of the young King Jehoash, which are found in 2 Kings xi. 4-16, and 2 Chron. xxiii. 1-15, you will be struck by some remarkable differences. As you will remember, the Queen Mother had, on the death of Ahaziah, slain all the male members of the royal family except the infant Jehoash, and had herself seized the kingdom. The young prince, who escaped the massacre, was kept in concealment until his seventh year, when, by the efforts of Jehoiada the High Priest, he was seated upon the throne, and the usurping queen was slain. The account in the book of Kings is as follows :

"And in the seventh year Jehoiada sent and

fetched the captains over hundreds of the Carites and of the Runners, and brought them to the House of Jehovah and made a covenant with them, and made them take an oath and showed them the king's son. And he commanded them saying: This is the thing ye shall do. The third part of you that come in on the Sabbath and keep the guard of the palace, . . . and the two parts of you that go forth on the Sabbath and keep the guard of the House of Jehovah [shall come] unto the king. And ye shall surround the king each with his weapons in his hand, and he that comes within the ranks shall be put to death, and ye shall be with the king when he goes out and when he comes in. And the captains of hundreds did according to all that Jehoiada the Priest commanded them. And they took each his men —those coming in on the Sabbath with those going out on the Sabbath, and came to Jehoiada the Priest (and the Priest gave them David's armour of state) and the Runners stood each with his weapons in his hand, from the south side of the House to the north side of the House, about the House and the altar, round about the king. And he brought out the king and placed upon him the diadem and the testimony and made him king and anointed him. And they clapped their hands and said : Long live the king ! "

The history here is so plain there can be no

mistaking. The principal actors are the officers of the body-guard with their men. This body of soldiers is divided, as was the case also in David's time, into three companies. These take their turn in guarding the temple and the palace, one-third being on duty at one point and two-thirds at the other. The Sabbath is the day when they exchange one post for the other, and it is probable that on that day, when the multitude at the temple is larger, two companies are on duty there, and only one company at the palace, while during the week the reverse is the case. Jehoiada, after showing the three centurions that the rightful heir to the throne is still alive, agrees that the company on duty at the temple, instead of going down to the palace, shall remain. When the other two companies come up from the palace, therefore, the whole body-guard will be around the young king, and Athaliah will be left without soldiers. The plan is carried out, and Athaliah, hearing the noise, comes unattended to the temple, because she has no soldiers at her command. This account, then, makes the matter the business of the body-guard, with which (except the High Priest) priests and people have nothing to do. How now does the Chronicler see the incident? In his account the Carites and Runners disappear. Jehoiada counsels indeed with certain captains of hundreds, but who they are does not distinctly appear. Instead of collecting troops, they go about the country and gather all the *Levites* and the heads of fathers' houses. It is a matter in which the whole people therefore take part. The account goes on :

" And all the congregation made a covenant with the king in the House of God. And he said unto them : Behold, the king's son shall reign as Jehovah hath spoken concerning the sons of David. This is the thing which ye shall do. The third part of you that come in on the Sabbath *of the Priests and of the Levites* shall be at the outer gates. And a third of you shall be *in the palace*, and a third part in the gate Jesod, and all the people shall be in the courts of the House of Jehovah. But let them not come into the House except the priests and those ministering to the Levites—they may come in because they are holy ; and let all the people keep the guard of Jehovah. And let the *Levites* surround the king each with his weapons in his hands, and he that cometh into the House shall be put to death, and let them be with the king when he cometh in and when he goeth out. And the *Levites* and all Judah did according to all that Jehoiada the Priest commanded."

Now it is perfectly clear that there is a discrepancy in the two accounts. In one, the main (in fact the only) actors besides Jehoiada are the royal guard. They come into the

temple, they surround the king, they guard him
and proclaim him king, and they kill Athaliah.
In the other account the body-guard is not
even mentioned.   The captains of hundreds
seem to be Levitical chiefs.   They gather the
Levites from the whole country.   *These* do
exactly what in the other account is attributed
to the mercenaries.   Yet in spite of the con-
spiracy being known to all the Levites and all
Judah, Athaliah has no inkling of it, and comes
unattended into the temple.   The account in
Kings is the original, and the deviations are
due to the point of view of the Chronicler.   In
the time before the exile, as we know from
various sources, there was no scruple (in practice, at least) against the entrance of foreigners
into the temple.   Ezekiel distinctly denounces
this as one of the customs of the time before
the captivity.   " Thus saith the Lord God : O
ye house of Israel, let it suffice you of all your
abominations in that ye have brought in aliens
uncircumcised in heart and uncircumcised in
flesh to be in My sanctuary to profane it when
ye offer My bread, the fat and the blood."   The
earlier kings, therefore, had guarded the temple
with their own troops.   But the stringency
with which the later Jews guarded the temple
from profanation made the Chronicler unable
to realise this ; especially that a High Priest
should have called upon the royal troops for
service in the temple seemed to him incredible.

He supposed the Levites must have been
called upon for this service, and hence he substituted them in the text.* It is clear that we
cannot ascribe freedom from error to the statements of a book compiled in this way. You
will say, then, it should be cast out of the
Canon. To which I reply, by no means. The
book of Chronicles is invaluable to us, not for
what it directly teaches, but for the light it
throws indirectly upon its own time. What
the Jews of the Persian monarchy were thinking, how they regarded the older history, how
they were preparing the way for the Scribes
and Pharisees, for the Crucifixion and the
Roman war, for the Talmud and Barkochba—
this is made known to us in the book of Chronicles, and by almost no other book of the Bible.
But it is made known to us by reading between
the lines; that is to say, by considering and

---

* As some questions have been raised by my assertions
about the Chronicler, I will add that of course I do not
suppose him guilty of intentional falsification of the
record. He had before him, it would appear, a considerable
literature which had commented on the history in the
spirit of the time—his changes are made from these documents. The ideas which govern this literature were a part
of the mental furniture of the Chronicler himself. His
inspiration, which made him a source of religious edification to his contemporaries, and which makes his work still
a part of the infallible rule of faith, *did not correct his
historical point of view* any more than it corrected his
scientific point of view, which no doubt made the earth
the centre of the solar system.

weighing not what the author says of others, but by what he betrays of himself. What is the truth of history, my friends? Is it simply the narrative of events definitely defined, and labelled, and arranged in order? Is it a catalogue of kings, of each of which it records that he was born, and made war, and died? Is it not rather a series of pictures, each of which describes an age with its thoughts, its aspirations, its ideals? If so, sacred history cannot be made up by a string of inerrant statements. It must show unconsciously, and by suggestion, the spirit that informs the Church of God, and makes it live and grow. To secure us an inerrant chronicle of dates and names would not give us this history. To give us the pictures of the men drawn by themselves is to give us this history. To discover these pictures, and to locate them, and set them in their true light, is the work of Biblical Theology working by criticism.

And now I must be prepared to hear an objection urged against the view here presented. If we cannot trust the Bible to be accurate in minor details we cannot trust it in anything. If we must give up one we must give up all. In reply to this I say, first, that a very large number of able and evangelical theologians do not admit this. Many of those who hold the most rigid theory of Inspiration say expressly that the admission of chronological or historical errors would not invalidate the infallible authority of the Bible. To substantiate this let me name Richard Baxter, who for himself says that he believes all errors now in the text to have come in by transmission. I quote from the " Reasons for the Christian Religion " the following :

" But those men who think that these human imperfections of the writers do extend further, and may appear in some by-passages of chronologies or history, which are no part of the rule of faith and life, do not hereby destroy the Christian cause. For God might enable His apostles to an infallible recording and preaching of the Gospel, even all things necessary to salvation, though He had not made them infallible in every by-passage and circumstance any more than they were indefectible in life. As for them that say, ' I can believe no man in anything who is mistaken in one thing, at least, as infallible, they speak against common sense and reason ; for a man may be infallibly acquainted with some things who is not so in all. A historian may infallibly acquaint me that there was a fight at Lepanto, . . . who cannot tell me all the circumstances of it. . . . I do not believe that any man can prove the least error in the Holy Scripture, in any point according to its true intent and meaning ; but if he could, the Gospel, as a rule of faith and life in things necessary to salvation, might be, nevertheless, proved infallible by all the evidences before given."* Without investigating a large number of theologians who are quoted † as making similar concessions, I will only call your attention to the fact that Christian Apologetic declares that the great things of Scripture can be proved without assuming the inerrancy of the record at all. President Patton, of Princeton, holds this view, as is well known. "I must take exception to the disposition on the part of some (he says) to stake the fortunes of Christianity on the doctrine of Inspiration. Not that I yield to any one in profound conviction of the truth and importance of the doctrine. But it is proper for us to bear in mind the immense argumentative advantage which Christianity has aside altogether from the inspiration of the documents on which it rests."‡ According to President Patton, then,

---

* *The Practical Works of the Rev. Richard Baxter,* London, 1830, Vol. XXI., p. 349.

† The author of the article, "Inspiration," in McClintock and Strong's *Cyclopædia*, says : "Others have gone so far as to avow that the value of the religious element in the revelation would not be lessened if errors were acknowledged in the scientific and miscellaneous matter which accompanies it. Among those who have held this form of the theory are Baxter, Tillotson, Doddridge, Warburton; Bishops Horsley, Randolph, and Whately, Hampden, Thirlwall, Bishop Heber, Dr. Pye Smith, Thomas Scott, and Dean Alford."

‡ Patton, *The Inspiration of the Scriptures,* p. 22.

so far from its being true that, unless the Bible be inerrant in every detail, we must give up its testimony to the matters of greater weight— so far from this being true, we might give up the inspiration altogether, and still have the assurance of these greater matters.

But, when a thing is said to be unthinkable, the best way to answer the assertion is to show that it has been thought. Some say they cannot conceive a Bible that can be relied on in matters of faith and morals, without making it infallibly true on points of chronology, history, and natural science. To this I reply: Many men have received the Bible, and do receive the Bible, as their infallible authority, who do not actually attribute to it, and who have not actually attributed to it, inerrancy in minor matters. This is true, as I have already said, of the Reformers. It is dangerous to cite a German in this connection. But the time was when Tholuck was honoured in America as a defender of the faith. Tholuck declared himself decidedly * against the absolute inerrancy of Scripture.

* In the article cited above. I might add here that among those who do not assert inerrancy, "but limit inspiration to such matters as directly pertain to the proper material of revelation, *i.e.*, to strictly religious truth," are to be found (according to McClintock and Strong) John Howe, Bishop Williams, Burnet, Lowth, Bishop Watson, Law, Barrow, Conybeare, Bloomfield, and others.

Among living theologians, Luthardt has earned the gratitude of the Protestant Church at large by his fruitful labours in varied fields of research. Luthardt declares that the older theology " certainly went too far." Van Oosterzee was, during his life, the representative of the orthodox party in the Reformed Church of Holland, yet he declares that " errors and inaccuracies in matters of subordinate importance are undoubtedly to be found in the Bible. A Luther, a Calvin, a Coccejus, among the older theologians ; a Tholuck, a Neander, a Lange, a Stier, among the more modern ones, have admitted this without hesitation."* And in our own country there has recently been published a book, by a careful investigator, which, while an able defence of "Supernatural Revelation," declines to assert inerrancy. † The author says : " As to the meaning of $\theta\epsilon\acute{o}\pi\nu\epsilon\upsilon\sigma\tau\sigma$ [in 2 Tim. iii. 16], there is not, and cannot, be any material difference of opinion. The chief difference relates rather to the object and degree of inspiration, whether it is the writings or the

* Van Oosterzee, *Christian Dogmatics*, 1. p. 205. It is worth noting that the latest defence of inerrancy comes from Germany, by Rohnert, noticed in *The Independent* of March 5, 1891.

† *Supernatural Revelation*: an Essay concerning the basis of the Christian Faith, by C. M. Mead, Lectures on the L. P. Stone Foundation, delivered at Princeton Theological Seminary.

writers that are inspired ; *and whether the inspiration secures absolute infallibility or not.* From the word itself, however, as Ellicott, Warrington, and others, properly insist, we cannot infer a verbal inspiration, such as the older theologians taught" (p. 299, sq. ; the italics are mine). Again, after defining the " deliverance of the Christian judgment in favour of the general and special trustworthiness of the New Testament in its descriptions [note !] of Christ and the Christian revelation," the author goes on to say : " Does this mean now that everything, without exception, that is found in the Scripture is to be accepted as absolute, unadulterated truth ? Is all critical inquiry into, the historical and scientific accuracy or logical soundness of Biblical utterances to be cut off? *By no means.* The Bible was written by imperfect and fallible men ; and it is only by the use of the rational and critical judgment that Christians have come to regard it of exceptional trustworthiness.

" If the same method of examination should reveal occasional instances of discrepancy and error, *this would be nothing more than* what might be expected, unless it has been demonstrated that the *writers were so inspired as to make them absolutely infallible.* But no such demonstration has ever been made " (p. 330 sq.).

But if you still feel that the concession of

minor errors endangers the spiritual truth, let
me ask you to notice the similar line of argument that might have been followed in the
past, but which has not actually resulted in
the overthrow of the Scriptures or of the
Church.

Suppose an inquirer comes to you with the
question how you know the Old Testament
Apocrypha not to be part of the Bible. You
explain to him the history of the Jewish Canon
and the testimony of the New Testament. He
asks, "Has the Church not actually accepted
these books as Scripture at some periods of its
history, and have not some eminent theologians
used them as the Word of God?" You will
be compelled to answer in the affirmative.
If, now, your inquirer says, "Well, if God
cannot guarantee His Word so that His
Church can tell exactly what it is, then I
cannot be sure that any of it is His," how
will you answer him? Surely you would not
admit that this uncertainty, even in a
matter of such importance as the extent of
the Canon, invalidates the Bible.

Or if a Bible student comes to you with
the Revised Version, and complains that the
Bible has been mutilated by the omission of
the passage concerning "three that bear witness in heaven," what will you do? You will
explain the process of transmission by manuscript. You will tell him that the verse is no

part of the original Scripture, but has crept into some copies by mistake. If now he says, "If God cannot secure His Word from errors of copyists, I cannot rely upon any part of it," what will you say? You will not admit this argument either, though it is precisely your own in case of admitted historical errors.

But, again, if one inquire why the Revised Version gives so many marginal renderings, some quite different from the text, you may be compelled to explain to him that the Hebrew is in some respects an imperfect language; that it has but two tenses, for example, so that the time of an action is often difficult to define as exactly as we should like ; that, moreover, the Hebrew script was at first very defective, and though it has been admirably supplemented by the system of points, yet there is reason to think the points sometimes in the wrong. After all this, he might take your line of argument and say, "If God could not express this revelation more accurately than that, I cannot depend upon it at all." But would he be right?

Now, all these are admittedly true. The Canon had no such authentication (so far as we know), as we should have insisted upon had it been a human document to be handed down as an authority. The text has not been preserved from error in transmission, and it was committed to a language of limited powers of expression and to a script peculiarly liable to ambiguity. But we all hold that it is, nevertheless, to us the infallible rule of faith and practice. If we suppose that the human factor, even in the autographs, showed traces of human fallibility, I do not see that that invalidates the rule of faith.

But now I want to call your attention to certain grave consequences of insisting that Inspiration implies absolute inerrancy. The first is, that this insistance may drive some to an utter rejection of the whole Revelation, because they suppose themselves to discover a single contradiction in the Scriptures themselves, or a single statement that conflicts with the established facts of natural science or of profane history. Dr. Evans has already alluded to this, and I will not enlarge upon it. Only it should be observed that the chances for error in the Old Testament are much greater than in the New Testament. The Old Testament took form in a cruder state of society, and its books cover a much greater period of time than is the case in the New Testament. We should naturally expect greater difficulties in the Old Testament. The caution exercised with regard to *a priori* theories in regard to the New Testament commends itself with double force when we come to the Old.

A second danger of insisting upon the doc-

trine of inerrancy is that it reverses the order
of the two principles of the Protestant Church.
As we have seen, the vital principle of the
Reformation was justification by faith. The
formative principle was the sufficiency of
Scripture as the rule of faith. If, now, you
invert them and put the Scripture first, do
you not endanger the faith in Christ? In
practice I do not believe this is done. If an
inquirer comes to a pastor, he is not met
with a demand to believe the Scripture to be
infallible in its every statement, but with the
exhortation to believe in the Lord Jesus
Christ, and this on the ground of the simple
historical testimony of the Scriptures as the
testimony of honest witnesses. But, is not
the central point in the Christian life the
central point in theology also? And I will
confess here the surprise with which I discovered what I think to be a grave defect in
the theology of the distinguished Dr. Hodge.
If you will read that author's discussion of the
subject of Faith you will acknowledge, I
think, that it suffers from just this defect.
Dr. Hodge defines faith as " the persuasion
of the truth founded on testimony," and then
adds : " The faith of the Christian is the persuasion of the truth of the facts and doctrines
recorded in the Scriptures on the testimony of
God." * A little later he says that the faith

* *Systematic Theology*, III., pp. 67, 68.

which secures eternal life " is founded not on the external or the moral evidence of the truth, but on the testimony of the Spirit with and by the truth to the renewed soul." Further on he gives the correct definition : " To believe that Christ is God manifest in the flesh . . . is to receive Him as our God. This includes the apprehension and conviction of His Divine glory and the adoring reverence, love, confidence, and submission, which are due to` God alone." But how this can be reconciled with the other definition I do not see. But suppose they mean the same thing. Dr. Hodge, as we have seen, declares all the assertions of Scripture free from error. If, now, faith is believing the facts and doctrines recorded in the Scriptures on the testimony of God, the life of faith becomes simply a mental effort to hold on to these facts. The young Christian studies his Bible and finds some things which seem to him contradictory. According to this theory, he must believe there is no error or he loses his Christian faith. He must hold on to the Bible (it will be said) no matter what science says or secular history, or the evidence of his own common sense. This is not the faith of Luther or of Paul or of the Shorter Catechism, which declares that " Faith in Jesus Christ is a saving grace, whereby we receive and rest upon *Him alone* for salvation as He is offered to us in the Gospel." What the pastor in his ministrations desires to awaken and foster in his converts is *this* faith in Jesus Christ.

All Scripture is God-inspired—true! But the remarkable thing is that the text affirms more than this. All Scripture is not only God-inspired, but all Scripture is "*profitable* for teaching, for reproof, for correction, for instruction, which is in righteousness; that the man of God may be complete, furnished completely unto every good work." This seems to me the hardest part of it. I find no difficulty in supposing the list of Dukes of Edom God-inspired, even though in the original autograph it had some names wrongly placed. But do you make it profitable for instruction in righteousness? Do you make it profitable * to yourself for completely fur-

---

* Everyone knows that the profitableness of all Scripture is not realized in ordinary Christian experience. A brilliant lecturer says that once, when eating a very fine shad, one of the company began to question him about his faith in Scripture. The questioner held up one difficulty after another and asked, " What do you do with this?" The reply was, "I treat it as I do the bones in my fish—I quietly lay it on one side." In practice, this is what everyone does. The soul does not *feed* on genealogical tables or lists of forgotten kings, no matter how strenuously it believes that they are all profitable for instruction in righteousness. Nor does the preacher make use of these in his work—though there is a tradition that a sermon was once preached on "the nine-and-twenty knives"

nishing yourself to every good work ?   If
not, you cannot lightly condemn me for not
drawing your deduction from its inspiration.
Surely, you would not allow me to censure
you for not practising upon your own confession of its profitableness. How to make
all Scripture profitable is at least as important
a question, and it is a more practical question
than how to establish its absolute inerrancy.

brought up from the captivity, and another on " the
night-hawk, the owl, and the cuckoo," from the list of
unclean birds. In practical Christian experience and
edification, some things in the Bible are quietly left at
one side.

Now, if a comparative anatomist were to study the shad,
the bones would become of the first importance to him.
It would hardly be necessary for the bystander to re-
monstrate with him for spending so much time on the
bones which contain no nutriment. But we, as students
of the Scripture, are precisely in this condition. We suppose the very things which the ordinary Christian may
quietly leave unused—we suppose these to throw light on
the *structure* of Scripture.   When we bring them forward
with this purpose, we are met by the assertion that these
cannot be what they seem to be—discrepancies cannot
exist. In other words, it is persistently asserted that
there can be no bones in the fish—that it is all good;
therefore we must swallow bones and all, or at least must
pound the bones fine by some reconciling hypothesis and
then declare them good meat.

The Lord Jesus at one time met the disciples when they
were hungry, and gave them a piece of fish broiled on the
coals. Were He to bring me such a gift, I should expect
to find it excellent fish. Should I, therefore, expect to
find it unlike any other fish in structure ? Would it be
disloyalty to Him to stop and look for the bones ?

And here is to the theological teacher the most serious question of all. To insist upon a constant assertion and defence of the inerrancy of Scripture is to turn the whole science of exegesis into a study of harmonistics. No doubt infidelity is constantly alleging contradictions and discrepancies that do not exist. For that reason, I would be slow to urge those which I suppose to exist. But to spend one's time in hypotheses designed to show how discrepancies *may* be reconciled is generally a fruitless task.

The truth frankly acknowledged is the truth's own best defence. But it is to be expected that we will discover some new truth. It is the duty of the special student to announce the discovery. That he will sometimes be hasty, sometimes will be one-sided, is to be expected. And it is to be expected that his positions will be attacked. It is desirable that they be attacked, for it is by discussion that the truth is advanced. I am sure no one in a theological chair in the Presbyterian Church could object to the sharpest discussion of his published views. Indeed, he would welcome it as a means of clarifying his own statements. But the discussion ought to discuss statements and not persons. In this revision year, we have heard much of the liberty given by the subscription to our standards. Is this a liberty to those

18

only who agree with us, to those only who do not believe the Pope of Rome to be an Antichrist, or even to those only who investigate the problems of theology "in order to vindicate the truth as held by our Church"? These questions must be answered by our pastors and elders, for they bear rule in the house of God. For one, I can say I want to have them answered rightly, not only for my own sake and the sake of the institution I serve, but for the sake of the whole Church of God, and for the sake of His truth. And so I end where my friend began. In order to progress there must be sympathy and confidence between pastors and professors. The work is one. Our aim is one. We must all account to the one Lord, " whose we are and whom we serve." May He help us to know His truth and to do His will !

LONDON :
W. SPEAIGHT AND SONS, PRINTERS,
FETTER LANE.

JAMES CLARKE & CO.'S BOOKS.

Pamphlets.

THE BEAUTY OF GOD, AND OTHER SERMONS. By T.
VINCENT TYMMS. Price 2d. 12s. per 100.

AN APPEAL TO YOUNG NONCONFORMISTS. Five Papers.
By R. F. HORTON, Hampstead. Price 2d. 12s. per 100.

A QUIET DAY FOR MINISTERS IN MANCHESTER. By
Rev. S. HARTLEY. An Address delivered in Besses Congre-
gational Church, Prestwich. Price 1d. 6s. per 100.

WHAT IS A CHRISTIAN CHURCH, AND WHY SHOULD I JOIN
ONE. By ERIC A. LAWRENCE. Price 2d.

THE NEEDS OF YOUNG MEN. By Archdeacon FARRAR.
Paper, 1d. ; or 3s. per 100.

PUBLIC MORALITY. By VOX CLAMANTIS. Reprinted in
pamphlet form from THE CHRISTIAN WORLD. 1. BETTING
AND GAMBLING—2. OUR STREETS—3. OUR AMUSEMENTS—
4. DRINK — 5. THE GETTING AND SPENDING OF MONEY.
One Penny each, or 3s. per 100.

THREE SERMONS BY DR. CLIFFORD.

THE PULPIT AND HUMAN LIFE ; or, the Minister as the
Interpreter and Spiritual Leader of Human Life. An Address
delivered to the Students of the Lancashire Independent
College, Manchester. Price Twopence.

THE OLD TESTAMENT IN THE TEACHING OF JESUS.
A Sermon preached at the Annual Meetings of the Baptist
Churches of the Midland Association, held at Wolverhampton.
Price Twopence.

COMING THEOLOGY. By J. CLIFFORD, M.A., D.D. Second
Edition. An Address from the Chair of the General Baptist
Association. Price 3d.

THE MORAL PIRATES, AND THE CRUISE OF "THE GHOST." With TWENTY-FIVE ILLUSTRATIONS. By W. L. ALDEN. Crown 8vo, cloth, 2s. 6d.

REEDHAM DIALOGUES. A Dozen Dialogues for Children. By late JOHN EDMED, Head Master of the Asylum for Fatherless Children, Reedham, Croydon. Eighth Thousand. Imperial 32mo, cloth, 1s. 6d.

WHAT OF THE NIGHT? A Temperance Tale of the Times. By MARIANNE FARNINGHAM. Fourth Thousand. Crown 8vo, Illuminated Cover, 1s.

THE BABY'S ANNUAL.

THE ROSEBUD ANNUAL FOR 1892. The Twelve Monthly Numbers of *The Rosebud*. In handsome cloth binding. Nearly 300 charming illustrations. Quarto, 4s.

DAILY CHRONICLE : *"The genial humour in which children take such delight distinguishes a large number of the tales, sketches, and rhymes ; and the illustrations, which reach a total of nearly three hundred, possess exceptional merit."*

PRESTON GUARDIAN : *" To many homes this book comes as a yearly visitor eagerly looked for by the children, whose expectations this year we are sure will be more than realised."*

One Volume Novels.

A MAN'S MISTAKE. By MINNIE WORBOISE. Crown 8vo, cloth, 5s.

ALL HE KNEW. A religious Novel. By JOHN HABBERTON, Author of " Helen's Babies," &c. Crown 8vo, cloth, 2s. 6d.

ROSLYN'S TRUST. By LUCY C. LILLIE, Author of " Prudence," " Kenyon's Wife," " The Household of Glen Holly." Crown 8vo, cloth, 3s. 6d.

" I have seldom, if ever, read a work of fiction that moved me with so much admiration."—GEORGE MACDONALD.

FOR THE RIGHT : A GERMAN ROMANCE. By EMIL FRANZOS. Given in English by JULIE SUTTER (translator of " Letters from Hell"). Preface by Dr. GEORGE MACDONALD. Crown 8vo, cloth, 3s. 6d. Third Edition.

DINAH'S SON. By L. B. WALFORD. Crown 8vo, cloth, 3s. 6d.

HAGAR : A NORTH YORKSHIRE STORY. By MARY LINSKILL, Author of " Between the Heather and the Northern Sea," " The Haven under the Hill," &c., &c. Crown 8vo, 1s.

LILLO AND RUTH ; or, Aspirations. By HELEN HAYS. Crown 8vo, cloth, 3s. 6d.

MERTONSVILLE PARK ; OR, HERBERT SEYMOUR'S CHOICE. By Mrs. WOODWARD. Fifth Edition. Crown 8vo, cloth, 5s.

CLARISSA'S TANGLED WEB. By BEATRICE BRISTOWE. Crown 8vo, cloth, 5s.

SISTER URSULA. By LUCY WARDEN BEARNE. Crown 8vo, cloth, 5s.

PRISCILLA ; OR, THE STORY OF A BOY'S LOVE. By CLARA L. WILLMETS. Cloth, 1s. 6d.

THE CATHEDRAL SHADOW. By MARIANNE FARN-INGHAM. Fifth Thousand. Crown 8vo, cloth, 3s. 6d. ; gilt edges, 4s.

THE SNOW QUEEN. By MAGGIE SYMINGTON. Third Thousand. Fcap. 8vo, cloth, 1s 6d. ; gilt edges, 2s.

BY AMELIA E. BARR.

"*Mrs. Barr's stories are always pleasant to read. They are full of sweetness and light.*"—SCOTSMAN.

"*In descriptive writing, in simplicity and gracefulness of style, and in perfect mastery over her characters, Mrs. Barr can hold her own with any living English novelist.*"—GLASGOW HERALD.

NOW READY.

FRIEND OLIVIA. Crown 8vo, 6s.

In a variety of handsome cloth bindings, or bound uniformly, crown 8vo.

THREE SHILLINGS AND SIXPENCE EACH.

In the Press. A SISTER TO ESAU.

SHE LOVED A SAILOR. *Just Ready*	IN SPITE OF HIMSELF
	A BORDER SHEPHERDESS
THE LAST OF THE MAC-ALLISTERS.	PAUL AND CHRISTINA
	THE SQUIRE OF SANDAL SIDE
WOVEN OF LOVE AND GLORY	THE BOW OF ORANGE RIBBON
FEET OF CLAY (*with portrait of author*)	BETWEEN TWO LOVES
	A DAUGHTER OF FIFE
THE HOUSEHOLD OF MCNEIL	JAN VEDDER'S WIFE

* A new and cheap edition of "JAN VEDDER'S WIFE" is now issued. In paper cover, price 1s. 6d.

THE HARVEST OF THE WIND, AND OTHER STORIES. By AMELIA E. BARR. Crown 8vo, paper, 1s.

NOVELS BY EMMA JANE WORBOISE.

NEW AND CHEAP EDITION.

*** *These Novels, which have hitherto been sold at Five Shillings each, are now issued at*

THREE SHILLINGS AND SIXPENCE EACH.

THORNYCROFT HALL	FATHER FABIAN
MILLICENT KENDRICK	OLIVER WESTWOOD
ST. BEETHA'S	LADY CLARISSA
VIOLET VAUGHAN	GREY HOUSE AT ENDLESTONE
MARGARET TORRINGTON	ROBERT WREFORD'S DAUGH-
THE FORTUNES OF CYRIL	TER
DENHAM	THE BRUDENELLS OF BRUDE
SINGLEHURST MANOR	THE HEIRS OF ERRINGTON
OVERDALE	JOAN CARISBROKE
GREY AND GOLD	A WOMAN'S PATIENCE
MR. MONTMORENCY'S	THE STORY OF PENELOPE
MONEY	SISSIE
NOBLY BORN	THE ABBEY MILL
CHRYSTABEL	WARLEIGH'S TRUST
CANONBURY HOLT	ESTHER WYNNE
HUSBANDS AND WIVES	FORTUNE'S FAVOURITE
THE HOUSE OF BONDAGE	HIS NEXT OF KIN.
EMILIA'S INHERITANCE	

The following 3s. 6d. Volumes are now issued at Three Shillings each.

MARRIED LIFE; OR, THE STORY OF PHILLIP AND EDITH.
OUR NEW HOUSE; OR, KEEPING UP APPEARANCES.

HEARTSEASE IN THE FAMILY	AMY WILTON
MAUDE BOLINGBROKE	HELEN BURY

BOOKS FOR THE HOLIDAYS. SPECIAL OFFER.

A limited number of the following Novels, published at FOUR SHILLINGS AND SIXPENCE, are now offered at TWO SHILLINGS AND SIXPENCE.

CAMPION COURT	SIR JULIAN'S WIFE
EVELYN'S STORY	THE LILLINGSTONES
LOTTIE LONSDALE	THE WIFE'S TRIALS